Into?

Into?

NORTH MORGAN

FLATIRON
BOOKS
NEW YORK

INTO? Copyright © 2016 by North Morgan. All rights reserved.
Printed in the United States of America. For information, address
Flatiron Books, 175 Fifth Avenue, New York, N.Y. 10010.

www.flatironbooks.com

The Library of Congress Cataloging-in-Publication Data is available upon request.

ISBN 978-1-250-14744-8 (hardcover)
ISBN 978-1-250-14745-5 (ebook)

Our books may be purchased in bulk for promotional, educational, or business use. Please contact your local bookseller or the Macmillan Corporate and Premium Sales Department at 1-800-221-7945, extension 5442, or by email at MacmillanSpecialMarkets@macmillan.com.

Originally published in Great Britain in 2016 by Limehouse
Books under the title *Love Notes to Men Who Don't Read*

First U.S. Edition: May 2018

10   9   8   7   6   5   4   3   2   1

To Brett Burbach and Michael Biagini

"Love is to share. Mine is for you."
—SÉBASTIEN TELLIER

"I am illuminated within by a diminishing light."
—JEAN-PAUL SARTRE

Into?

ARE YOU JEALOUS OF US?

The world closed in on me, so I had to get out. On Saturday, having packed as much as I can into two large suitcases, I make my way to Heathrow where I catch a flight heading west. This must look like an act of surrender, telling both of them that they won, though this isn't a war. This, to me, is a way of figuring out what the hell happened, but in a different city, one where I won't feel humiliated.

During the three weeks after everything fell apart, but when I was still in London and living with my now ex-boyfriend Brett, it becomes abundantly clear to me that Brett and Frank are still very much seeing each other, going on dates, attending dinner parties as a couple. During these weeks, I also find out that Frank has a boyfriend that he lives with, who remains unaware of everything.

I contact the boyfriend and tell him what has been happening. The boyfriend refuses to believe me. I contact Brett and tell him about the boyfriend. Brett refuses to believe that the boyfriend exists. Brett contacts Frank and enquires about the boyfriend. Frank responds that there is a boyfriend but they've broken up. I message the boyfriend to confirm that they're still together, get a written response saying, "Yes, Frank and I are together," take a screenshot and forward it to Brett. A week later, I get a message from the boyfriend telling me that I was right and that he has now broken up with Frank. Just to sum up: me and the boyfriend out. Brett and Frank in.

Just to sum up further: my boyfriend of four years whom I live with now has a new boyfriend. A boyfriend who also has another boyfriend. Someone I've hooked up with in the past before I met my boyfriend and he met his boyfriend.

This is who we are. This is my social group. We are gays living in big metropolitan areas heavily involved in the scene. We all know each other. We all have big muscles and violent abs and handsome faces and lots of disposable income and innumerable sexual partners, each one hotter than the last. We adopt variations of heteronormative looks (some of us are bros, some of us are jocks, some of us are simply worked-out guys-next-door), which we document incessantly on Facebook, Instagram, and all your other surrounding news feeds and timelines. We will post pictures with our shirts off, standing together on party dance floors or next to expensive hotel swimming pools, and sometimes we'll even quote *Mean Girls* and caption the picture with "You can't sit with us." We go to the best parties, take the best drugs, and have VIP tickets for the best events. We don't even pay for them. Are you jealous of us?

In order to attract the right kind of attention, we will publicly maintain that this isn't who we really are. We don't want this. We'll say that we really want to settle down. We'll say that we want to start a family. We'll say that we find this kind of lifestyle empty, unfulfilling, and horribly temporary. Who wants to be a messed-up, single gay guy, going from gay bar to gay pride, we'll say, with nothing else of substance going on in his life? We will very carefully curate our public image to show how wholesome we are, and will balance out the pictures of our beautiful, half-naked friends with pictures of our baby nephews (nieces are much less popular) taken in bulk in the two hours every six months that we get to see them.

We fall in love with each other and we move in together, and retire from the scene for a few months, maybe a couple of years, because we have found happiness, and we don't need this any longer; we're over it. Then we fuck things up for fun or because we're bored, and we start going out again and seeing all the people we know—most of them are still there at a different stage of their own cycle—and we fall right back into place and we do it all over again.

We can have this forever. All that changes is that each time you go back there's one more person at the party that you have to avoid making eye contact with, or dancing too close to, because in the very recent past you destroyed their soul a little bit, or they destroyed yours.

MARCH

1

My name is Konrad Platt and I have now been in America for eight days. This is a homecoming of sorts, as I was actually born here. My father is American. My mother is German. I lived here for only the first four years of my life and then moved to Berlin with Mum, after my parents' divorce, so we could be close to her family and she could get help bringing me up. Dad still lives in Pacific Palisades, California, where I am right now, and though we talked on the phone and did see each other once or twice a year when I was growing up, we've never been that close and he doesn't know much about what's happening in my personal life. He doesn't know that I'm gay, for one thing. It's not that he doesn't care, though I'm sure he does not, it's primarily that all this was a long time ago—it was 1984 when Mum and I moved to Europe—he's been remarried since, has had two more children with his second wife, and I'm just part of a barely mentioned history. About five years ago, I started working for him remotely from Europe (he owns an independent private wealth management firm), and even though our contact became much more frequent professionally, this never extended to our personal relationship.

When I was sixteen, I moved from Berlin to London, because it seemed exciting and because I wanted to. I took my A levels there and then on to UCL, where I studied financial risk management. I worked for a couple different finance companies in London for a few years before taking the easy way out and going to work for Dad. I have only a handful of clients whose portfolios I help manage, and most of my day is spent reading, researching, compiling information, and seeing how I can help make rich people even richer. The good thing is that I can work remotely from anywhere I want, and I don't have to talk to anyone on a daily basis.

I came out in an uneventful way in my last year at university. It was London and nobody cared. My mum and her family didn't care either. I did have some very predictable clichéd issues that tortured me for a few years before doing so, and I did spend some time viewing myself as a tragic figure, fighting internal battles, trying to overcome perceived adversity, but those are feelings everyone tends to have and then eventually you manage to get over yourself.

So when I was in my second year at university I moved into a house share with three of my friends and we would all go out a lot and get drunk and all those guys would bring girls back home and sleep with them all the time, but I didn't do any of that, seeing that I had never had sex, and I think I might have kissed a total of three girls in my life but not for very long, and the idea was freaking me out. I thought I would never come out and I was planning to lead a pseudostraight life, probably celibate.

When I had nothing to do, I would sometimes take the Tube and go to Soho on my own and walk around a bit. And I would walk past gay shops and bars and bookstores, but I wouldn't dare walk in. Later that year, I would sometimes get the courage and I would go in and look at magazines and DVDs on the shelves, but I wouldn't pick them up, because I was scared I would draw attention to myself and somebody might see me from outside.

Around that time I decided that maybe I wanted to go ahead and meet a guy. I started going on an online dating site that is now long gone, and I made a profile and put some pictures up, without showing my face. I was telling myself that I would meet somebody once, sleep with him, and then I would get this out of my system and be straight. I spent about four months talking to people on there and trying to find somebody that seemed like a decent person to do this with. I bought a laptop to go online with and I kept it hidden from my housemates behind a cupboard that I actually had to physically move to access, as if having to move a piece of furniture a few inches before accessing an online world of available men would be an actual barricade to acting on my sexuality.

One Friday in April, I met a guy. He was seven to eight years older than me with a dumb, square face and a thick neck and a big, hairy chest and I couldn't get past typing a whole sentence to him on my laptop without getting hard. I didn't go to classes and I lied to my friends that I was going away for the day. I was meeting him at 11:00 A.M. and I was completely terrified, so I downed two beers and some vodka before I left home. I met him, we had coffee, I lied to him about my name, my age, where I'm from, what I did, everything. He was nice enough to pretend to believe me when I was telling him that I didn't want to be gay, this would only be a one-off experience and I would never come out. We went back to his place and had sex.

I didn't tell anyone anything for another five months. The first person I told was Ben, my best friend from UCL. We were in some bar in Holborn after the summer break and the song that was playing was "Silver Screen Shower Scene" by Felix da Housecat featuring Miss Kittin, which has nothing to do with me coming out but I remember it very specifically, and I told Ben I had something to say and I started crying because I thought he would never want to talk to me again and then I told him. It took another month until I told the second person, and that was one of my other housemates. By the Christmas break of my third year at Uni, I had told all my friends in London.

I met Brett at an after club in North London over four years ago. He was interesting, handsome, and he was a born and bred Londoner, which was very important to me at the time because I wanted to have roots in this city. At the same time, I wasn't really looking for a relationship. I was quite content with my love life—there were enough people in London to fuck, mess around with, lead on, and get led on by, but I don't suppose you can choose when these things will happen. Brett had had a dramatic breakup just a few weeks before meeting me. He was looking around more actively than I was, trying to meet somebody else and get over the ex. We slept together the first night, of course, but then uncharacteristically kept seeing each other. We became boyfriends a few weeks later. The following year, we moved in together. In the four years that we were together, at first we went out a lot. Then we stayed in a lot. We traveled together. I spent time with his family. He flew to Berlin with me often to visit my mum. We were monogamous. We got bored of monogamy and had threesomes. We felt bad about having threesomes and became monogamous again. We fought and broke up and got back together again and we got a puppy. We talked about getting married. We were gay.

During the last year of the relationship things had changed a bit, though. There was a general sense that perhaps Brett didn't love me as much as I loved him. It felt like he was losing interest. But it's easier to recognize that now, in retrospect, knowing exactly how things ended.

In the eight days that I've lived in my dad's house in the Palisades, I haven't once actually left the pool house where I'm staying. I'm having a wonderful time sobbing, staring blankly into space in what I believe is a hugely dramatic way, not listening to sad breakup music because I'm too upset even to do that, researching methods of a painless suicide (there are none, nothing is as effortless as you want it to be unless you have a gun, and even that's not guaranteed to put you out of your misery), and looking at every picture that Brett and his new boyfriend post online, and they're taking many because they're very proud and want to show each other off. My dad and his wife, who hardly know me that well anyway and don't know the reasons why I decided to pick up and move across the world and into their place all of a sudden, must think that I'm completely insane. The fact that I'm spending most of my time heavily medicated (steady doses of Vicodin, Xanax, and Valium in the daytime to help me ease the pain, experimental combinations of Zopiclone and Ambien at night to help me sleep) really mustn't help.

2

Last Sunday, I moved to West Hollywood. I know only one person who lives in LA apart from my dad and his family, a kid called Anthony who's twenty-four, from London, and moved here a couple of months ago. Well, I know a few other people because I've met them at parties around the world, but Anthony is the only one that I've spent any time one-on-one with and have lived in the same city as, before. Anthony is short, maybe around five nine, unnaturally muscular, with a marine haircut and covered in badass tattoos. I realize I just described everyone who has stepped foot in a gay bar in the Western Hemisphere in the last five years. From what I understand Anthony left London to come check out LA because he was bored, and now he's moved in with a rich stoner guy called Markus, who's funding his lifestyle and their mutual drug habit. In his spare time from doing nothing at all, Anthony dances on a forty-inch-by-forty-inch podium in a bar on Santa Monica Boulevard.

When Anthony found out the details of my breakup, he

insisted that the only way I'm going to feel better is if I put an end to my self-imposed isolation at my dad's pool house and move to WeHo to fuck some new people and start moving on. My emotional state is such right now that I'll happily take serious life advice from an aimless go-go dancer, so I found a one-bedroom apartment, packed up my bags, and moved.

On Friday, I finish work and I drive to the gym like I have done every day this week. Getting ready to go lift some weights can be a very stressful process, in terms of how you have to look, but at the end of the day all you have to do is be observant and copy what the straight guys are wearing. Some basketball shorts, a loose fitting T-shirt from your college days, a pair of black sports socks pulled up high, and a wristband or two to show that you lift very hard and have injured yourself, and you're all set.

In the lift on the way up to the gym from the parking garage there are two bros in gym clothes and an old lady, who must be going to the Whole Foods next to the gym.

She looks up at them wearing full douche bag attire, including sweatbands around their heads, and says:

"Are you boys going to the gym?"

The one gym bro who's hotter and looks like more of a dick smirks and says, "Yeah."

Then the old lady continues:

"To exercise and get buff?"

He laughs and says "yeah" again.

"And get those six-pack abs?"

Then the gym bro lifts his shirt up and says, "I already have those," and I want both to kill him and jerk off on his stomach. Then the lift gets to the gym floor and we all get out.

Today I'm working out my shoulders. In the gym, there's a boy whom I've seen every time I've come here, always in the evening, always with a friend of his (invisible to me), and the thing about this boy, who cannot be any older than nineteen, maybe twenty, is that he's tall and blond, and has a toned body, fine, but he also has a pair of blue eyes that have that effect on me where if they catch mine, my heart stops for a moment and I have to take a second to remember (a) where I am and (b) what I am doing. This is not an effect to be taken lightly and it takes a very particular shade of blue for it to happen. The fact that his eyes look like they've witnessed an impossible tragedy, and will never recover, only adds to it. So because this feeling that I get when I look at him in the eyes is very, very disturbing, but also very exhilarating, I can't help but seek it out. And I keep staring at him. Because I keep staring at him, he tends to look back, and to cut a long story short, when this boy is in the gym, nothing really gets done. Not that I want anything from this boy, other than to occasionally get the electric shock he seems to be able to readily inflict on my nervous system.

Now, apart from my own personal fetish for arctic blue eyes that reflect centuries of endless sorrow, this boy is also overwhelmingly good-looking objectively. And I stand there and look at him and keep thinking of the time when it will all come together four or five years from now and he's turned into an actual god, and how he will deal with his life then, a life where everyone around him will be falling over themselves to make things easy for him and get close to him and take advantage of him. A life in the bubble that those extraordinarily good-looking people live in and the rest of us bastards will never experience.

Then I go back home, and it's Friday evening and Anthony comes over with Markus and they want to go out. Well, Anthony wants to go out. Markus is too stoned to care either way.

"You're coming out with us," Anthony says.

"I'm not going anywhere."

"And why's that?"

"Because I don't feel like it."

"So you're gonna stay in and be lonely and depressed?"

"Yes, that sounds excellent. I'll do that."

"Well, you're never going to feel better if you keep doing that," he snarls at me.

Then Markus tells him to leave me alone and then the two of them do a line of coke on a dish in the kitchen and then go out.

I start watching the first movie that shows up as I'm flicking through the channels. It stars some big-name white American actors and a number of unknown Indian actors and appears to be all about prejudice, integration, cultural assimilation, and the surprising enormity of the human spirit, but I'm not really paying any attention. Instead I keep thinking of Brett in London and missing him and reminiscing about all our time together and wondering what we would be doing on this Friday night if we were still together like we were two months ago and trying to guess what he's doing right now with someone else instead, so eventually I turn off the TV and make a half-assed attempt at meditating and clearing my head because someone advised me to do that, but I don't really know how to meditate, so this results in me staring blankly at the wall for the next two hours or so, and then I fall asleep.

3

On Saturday I go out to meet some friends for one of their friends' birthday, and I'm using the term "friends" in a delusional way, because I don't really know anyone in LA. These are Anthony's friends. I don't know that LA is filled with people who want to be my friends anyway; I think I'm too intense and gloomy even in my most upbeat moments, and nobody has time for that here. Here, even in just one week I've met people who tell me that they're writers and they love Kafka, but in subsequent conversation I discover that they've never blacked out or fallen in a k-hole in their lives, I mean how is that even possible, or people who read back to me the cover of the book I'm holding and pronounce Proust "Praust," as in "Faust." There's nothing wrong with not liking Kafka, of course, and not knowing how to pronounce Proust, but please stop pretending.

The birthday boy is called Rus. He's in a threesome relationship with Daniel and X, an actually very famous actor who's not openly gay to the public. Daniel has a ton of money and a huge dick, and these are the first two things that anyone will tell you about him. Rus is the epitome of black male beauty, combining a mid-1990s Tyson Beckford with the body intensity of a hundred-meter Olympic sprinter. Of course he doesn't work, because why would you work if you were going out with a rich entrepreneur and a Hollywood movie star?

We end up at some warehouse party in downtown LA and it's boring and nobody in my group pretends that this was a smart choice, but some of them become more easily accustomed than others because they're better at finding pills. One of those friends is Rus, who's really quite high at the point when he comes up to me and puts his arms around my waist.

"Konrad," he says into my ear. "We're so happy that you've moved here. Everyone here likes you."

"Aw, thanks, man. I like you guys too."

"You have to be careful though."

"What do you mean?"

"I know you're new here. And LA is a great place to be. But you don't want to be sucked into the gay scene."

He pulls back for a few seconds and puts something in his mouth. Then comes back to kiss me and slips a pill into my mouth with his tongue.

"Just be careful. That's all some people do with their lives."

And I find that upsetting, because, well, how do I tell him that his warning has arrived too late? How do I tell him I was sucked in several years ago and am still trying to find a way out? When I came out at twenty and started going to these places I used to think I'd never be doing this at thirty. I'm thirty-three and, still, here I am. But as you get older, your self-imposed timeline keeps getting extended. Right now, can I really set my gay scene getaway at thirty-five with any sort of conviction? What about forty? Can I promise to myself that I won't be forty-two and crawling around some gay party with my shirt off?

Gay men like me never grow old. Out of all those men in the suburbs, leading the dreary lives that I so want, maybe some used to go out. Maybe some had been sucked in and they managed to escape. But I think that most of them never got involved in the first place. Not to the extent that I have and the people around me have. The likes of me will continue to live in central London, LA, New York, or wherever and find ourselves in clubs on Saturday nights at 4:00 A.M., kissing each other pills passing around delayed and pointless advice about getting sucked in.

4

The one good thing that is happening in my life right now is that I have finally figured out the training schedule of the hot straight guys in my gym. And now I can shift my life around that and "accidentally" turn up at the same time. There is a group of around six or eight of them and they may not all be there consistently working out together always, but if you go between the hours of 8:30 P.M. and 10:30 P.M. on any given night, you will find at least three or four. This is a bit late in the day and it intervenes with one's dinner plans and sleeping needs, but luckily I have neither of those, so I'm there.

Like any clique, this one has its own rules, behavioral modes, and hierarchies. Some of the bros are more outgoing. Some are quieter. Some are more submissive. And there is one clear leader. Despite their individual roles and idiosyncrasies, there are two stable factors that apply to the group as a whole: (a) they only talk to each other and dismiss everyone else in the gym, and (b) there is not a single one of them I would not fuck.

My love affair with the group started in the locker room

toilets, although unfortunately this is not as crude as it first sounds. You can tell a lot about a man's place in the world by the way he behaves at a public urinal. As a homosexual with confidence issues, taking a piss at a urinal is already a huge challenge for me. I'll always choose the cubicle if there is one, but if not, I will go for the urinal that's as far away as possible and I will stand there for minutes trying to force myself to go, playing various mental games as a distraction while at the same time praying that nobody else shows up next to me. If someone does and he's straight, eight out of ten times he will arrive, get his dick out, start pissing like it's fucking nothing, finish, shake it off, slap it back in, and walk away all in the same time that I've been standing there next to him holding mine and counting the tiles in front of me in the faint hope that *something* will start streaming out of it as I slowly die of embarrassment. Because, you know . . . he knows what's happening. He can hear the silence.

Two weeks ago, some meathead stood at the urinal next to me and started peeing using only one hand while employing the other one to pick sunflower seeds out of his basketball shorts' pocket and transfer them into his mouth where he cracked the shells open before spitting them out. I knew that I had no chance. I was in love. Imagine the confidence of being able to pee at the urinal uninterrupted as if no one else is around, but please, take a minute and imagine the confidence of doing this very thing while eating. This man was some sort of god. The fact that this endeavor may have been kinda filthy was not detrimental to my carnal attraction to him. He could have brought in a trash can and emptied it there for all I care. I probably would have liked him more.

After that, I followed the guy to the gym floor. He led me to my now beloved group of douche bag straight bros, and I haven't looked back since.

On this Wednesday evening, sunflower seeds, the leader, is there with three of his subordinates, plus the addition of a blond girl, who seems to be his girlfriend. She is Christina Aguilera straight out of the "Dirrty" video. I know that's from fifteen years ago, but in certain parts of Southern California it's considered a classic, timeless look. As part of a plan to attract all the attention he can possibly get (even though his just existing there immobilized in a tank filled with formaldehyde like Damien Hirst's shark would be more than enough for me), the leading gym meathead is performing an impossible, completely useless, and highly dangerous task with a forty-five-pound barbell.

He is lying on the floor flat on his back. Next to him is the barbell with added forty-five-pound weight plates on each side. With one hand, he grabs the bar in the middle and slowly sits up, then eventually stands up with his arm extended up over his head, holding the 135-pound weight in perfect balance. One of the subordinates and his girlfriend are filming this on their phones. All three of the men watching are shouting encouraging comments like, "Yeah buddy!" and "Get it, boy." When this is done, they all cheer. The leader puts the weight on the floor and kneels down to allow his girlfriend to climb on his shoulders. He lifts her up, and they both flex their biceps while two of the subordinate males take more pictures.

When I go home later in the evening, even before stalking Brett and his new boyfriend online, I open Instagram and search by the gym geotag. Sure enough, I find two posts: the video of the weight lift has been posted by one of the other bros and the picture with the girlfriend on the shoulders has been posted by the girlfriend. The meathead that I like is tagged in both. I check his profile but there isn't much on there. I then check the girlfriend's. She has over five hundred posts and every single one of them includes the hashtag #savedbyLA. She has many pictures with her gym boyfriend, in several of which he is shirtless (they seem to like the beach), even though the relationship appears to be only three or four weeks old. In her latest post, the one of her sitting on his shoulders, she has commented, "His love roared louder than her demons." I don't understand any of it. How was this Christina Aguilera lookalike saved by LA? What were her demons? I have demons. Where is my gym meathead? Who's going to save me? I follow both of them and go to bed.

5

The next morning I wake up. I am unhappy. It was such a smart idea to run away from London and try to get over my heartbreak in a whole new city where I don't know anyone. Seeing that I don't have anyone to talk to in real life, I go online. After my usual check-in with Brett's social media so that I get that daily stab in the heart, I start wasting time reading about music.

I spend a lot of time on an online message board called Popjustice, where hundreds of people discuss and analyze pop stars and pop music relentlessly with forensic attention to detail and almost terrifying dedication. All those hundreds of people are gay and the music that they like is primarily big commercial pop, like Lady Gaga and Rihanna and Britney Spears. Sometimes male pop stars too, and sometimes more obscure pop, but mainly pop fronted by all-singing, all-dancing powerful females. Those guys live for this type of music. They listen to it, watch it, then go on the Internet and spend hours talking about it. They even use a very specific vernacular to talk about pop music and to each other, a lot of which is borrowed from ball culture, as seen in *Paris Is Burning*, and has more recently been widely popularized by *RuPaul's Drag Race* and the Internet overall. On the Popjustice message board, there is always a young gay guy whose wig has been snatched by a new pop video that just dropped, and there's always a young gay guy who is spilling the tea on a pop album that's about to leak.

I have absolutely no interest in listening to the music that these people talk about, and I don't necessarily think that it's because my internalized homophobia extends that far. I just like alternative music, mainly, and have done so since I was thirteen years old and discovering the Smiths, New Order, Suede, and other bands like that. However, this is literally the most visited website on my Internet browser outside social media and porn. And despite not caring at all about the music they discuss, I care very much about the way that they do it and the things that they say. I love it so much when Beyoncé appears on a red carpet somewhere and a thousand twinks go online and declare that *she's giving them life*. I love it so much when Mariah Carey does a live performance and *murders* a note and half of the posters are *slain* by her anyway and the other half tear her apart.

A lot of the time, most of the time, I don't even listen to the songs or watch the performances they talk about, but I just log on and read their hyperreactions. I guess that no matter how masculine I want to appear on the outside and how turned on I become by any moronic pseudobro with steroid muscles and a backward baseball cap, deep inside me there is a very girly, very repressed fag that is dying to find someone to relate to. So I read and I read and I read about Kylie Minogue's Christmas album and Britney Spears's Las Vegas residency and the pre-chorus to Ariana Grande album tracks that I'll never hear and it warms my little broken gay heart.

6

On this Friday, my friend William comes to visit from London on his way to Australia. We are all very international, and we can't settle for one country. Even limiting yourself to one continent is just laughable; circuit parties happen just about everywhere.

William's visiting and staying at my place, and while I'm pushing for a nice weekend catching up on some *Frasier*, maybe a stroll down to the local park, William has big plans to go out and cannot be convinced otherwise. I mean, I've always been kinda boring and a bit of a difficult person to get on with, but now because I'm heartbroken and have unjustly chosen to blame the scene for everything that happened to me, I must be truly insufferable to hang out with.

William has two modes: either studying hard for some upcoming medical exam, during which time he won't pick up the phone to see how you are, or, when the exam is over, party party party. These days I have two modes also: watching *Frasier*, or being dragged out and ruining everyone else's good

time by insisting we go back. Thankfully for William, everyone else I know in this city through Anthony has one mode
only and that is party party party party. That's one more "party"
than William.

Because we're in LA and it's a Saturday, we are invited to a
pool party. Well, Anthony and Markus are invited, but William and I are also allowed to go because we've already been to
the gym six times this week.

The pool party is in Los Feliz. I have no idea whose house
this is, but when the four of us arrive, it's already packed. There
must be at least eighty people there. I hardly know any of them
but recognize a few from Instagram and other online sources.
We lose Anthony and Markus pretty quickly, because they
have to make the social rounds, but William stays with me.
The next half hour or so plays out like this:

- William and I watch the WeHo gays from a distance
- The WeHo gays watch William and me from a
  distance
- Everyone chooses who they want to fuck
- William finally convinces me to join Anthony and
  Markus in the pool

Our friend group now has a new recruit, whose name is not
important, but what is important is that he has the best circuit
body at the party and that Anthony really wants to have sex
with him. This seems to be causing quite a lot of aggravation to
Markus, who's spending his time making gestures to Anthony
to keep his hands to himself, or he might just end up having
sex with this person right in this pool in front of everyone.

It's now around 5:00 P.M. I get out of the pool to go snort stuff in the bathroom with Markus, and when I come back Anthony and Circuit Body have moved into one of the hot tubs away from the pool. Circuit Body is sitting on the side with his legs in the water, and Anthony is standing between said legs facing him directly. Their faces are about two inches away from each other. Markus walks over casually (not casually at all) and asks whether they've kissed yet. They both say no. I believe that as much as Markus does. We sit on either side of Circuit Body and catch up on their conversation. They are discussing sexual positions. Anthony wants the three of them to go inside the house and find an empty bedroom. Markus turns down the plan, tells Anthony that it's time to go, and the group that I came with—Anthony, Markus, and William—all leave.

In the evening, Markus is still mad at Anthony, so Anthony, William, and I go and meet a friend of William's named Scott. Scott lives up in the Hollywood Hills and has a fantastic view of the city, so we just stay inside and get stoned. The edible that I had is making me very lethargic, I can barely stand up, but I'm having an OK time tying and untying my Sperry shoelaces over and over again. Everyone else is watching funny YouTube videos projected onto a wall from Scott's laptop.

"Oh my god," shouts Anthony. "I know what we should do."

He turns to William and asks, "Have you ever been to Palm Springs?"

"Actually, I haven't."

"Oh my god, oh my god. We have to go to Palm Springs for the weekend."

"It's nearly midnight on Saturday night. You can't be making plans to go away this weekend. The weekend is nearly gone," I say.

"Well, you never want to do anything anyway," says Anthony. He asks William again, "Do *you* want to go?"

"Sure. That sounds like fun."

I force myself to get up and go to the bathroom and when I come back they have already booked a hotel for the next day. In the morning, we find ourselves driving down to Palm Springs.

We spend the Sunday by the hotel pool, because there is genuinely never anything else to do in Palm Springs, and in the evening we go over to somebody's house party, a Tom or an Evan, where the main event is a huge outdoor screen by the swimming pool playing the film *Showgirls*. Because, you know, it's trashy. We love trashy things, but most of all trashy celebrities. Lindsay Lohan, right? Isn't she such a mess? She has a drug addiction and is throwing her life away. We'd never do that. We've got our lives together. Let's ironically worship Lindsay instead.

The highlight of this house party is when two guys jump in the pool and re-create the bad sex scene between Elizabeth Berkley and Kyle MacLachlan from the film (lots of screaming, writhing, splashing around) as it plays on the big screen. A lot of people are filming or taking pictures of this on their phones, and when it's done, everyone erupts into wild applause. Shortly after, I get an Uber and go back to the hotel by myself.

7

On Wednesday I start my day with my part-time occupation of scrolling through Instagram and looking at hot guys that I never want to have anything to do with in real life because they seem like jerks, plus they might not even talk to me anyway.

My first discovery of the day is a guy called Shawn, who lives in Boston. Shawn is thick as fuck and has a shaved head and a blond fuzzy beard. His face is practically square, and just by looking at him I really want him to head-butt me and leave me bleeding on the ground outside after I mistakenly touched his hand while ordering a beer at the crowded bar, which he took as a sign that I'm some fag hitting on him.

Shawn appears to be spending his time uploading videos on Instagram of him performing CrossFit exercises without a shirt on and adding commentary like, "Getting my jump rope skills ready for the @CrossFit metcon. Can't wait to PR this weekend on my lifts #liftoff #crossfitgames #liftheavy #nobelt #epicresults" and "305# x 2 Push Press." I can't decipher this highly advanced code, but it's really turning me on, whatever the hell it means. He also seems to make a living by selling personalized workouts and diet programs to his 45.4k followers, all of which I can get for free on any random bodybuilding message board after spending two seconds online. But somehow, somewhere stupid people exist that prefer to send their money to Shawn and get them from him.

I review Shawn's profile and admire how much of an asshole and how straight he is, but the further I go into his 695 posts that date back to three years ago, the more suspicious I get. The CrossFit doesn't start until sixty-five weeks ago, the beard doesn't appear until ninety-seven. Long before the videos of him mouthing "Bitch you guessed it, hoo, you woz right" to some rap song playing while he's doing squats in the gym, I find a video of him singing along to something that sounds to me conspicuously like a musical number with his own voice . . . and he sounds good. Bros don't ad lib to "Defying Gravity" from *Wicked*.

So I take this investigation to Google and start searching his name. And I am devastated to find that Shawn, before the steroids and facial hair, was a minor Broadway actor. I am even more devastated to find that he was pretty much openly gay until the musical career disintegrated and the times changed, of course, and he had to move back to Boston from New York and reinvent himself as an aggressively heterosexual online personal trainer.

Just before my attraction to him disappears completely, I am blessed by some sort of divine inspiration and type his name into Google followed by the word "naked." Ten minutes later I have downloaded and jerked off to two videos of him that someone has saved from the time when Shawn was selling live webcam shows, presumably to fund himself between his two careers. I unfollow him on Instagram, because there's nothing to put you off a straight bro faster than seeing him type "Tip me" when the webcam-show client has asked him to bend over and finger himself (which he does), but I save the videos to watch again in the future, because I'm a hypocrite and the attraction hasn't gone at all.

8

On Thursday morning around 4:00 A.M. I'm lying in bed think-ing violent thoughts about Brett and his new boyfriend, Frank, and I guess the universe must have heard me and wanted to give me an update, because a message pops up on my Facebook messenger. It's from Simon, a London acquaintance who I probably last saw over a year ago. Despite us not being good friends at all, Simon seems very concerned.

"Hey, Konrad, I was wondering how you're doing over there in the U.S. Did you hear about Brett and Frank getting engaged? I'm sorry mate. Hope you're having an OK time. Are you dating anyone new?"

OK, well, now I'm wide-awake plus there seems to be a sudden oxygen shortage in the room, so I step out on the bal-cony to get some air. Simon, you little bitch, I'm thinking. I'm also thinking maybe this isn't true, maybe he's just making this up. I check Brett's social media but can't see any evidence, and message Simon back.

"I heard this yeah. It's all good, man—they're dating, I'm

sure they can do what they want. I'm fine. It's really fun being in LA."

Simon writes something back but I don't even look at it. I find a video of a drugged-up threesome Brett and I had with some Dutch guy after London Pride a couple of years ago, watch the whole ninety minutes, jerk off twice, and go back to bed.

9

Almost three months into living in the U.S., I am starting to understand what's up. At some point in the last five years, "bro," the movement in which affirming your masculinity means emulating the appearance and behavior of twenty-two-year-old frat boys, overtook "urban" as the predominant aspirational youth culture in America. I don't know why it happened. It happened. I remember when everyone was trying to be all gangsta when I was living in London in my early twenties. Well, now everyone wants to be just a chill bro. Chillen the eff out. Chillen the eff out at Coachella, sports games, maybe the old tailgate. With Bud Light. Chill AF.

These cultural trends don't bypass the gays, of course. We all want to belong. We'll latch on to whatever fad comes along. Bring them on. In fact, we won't just latch on. We'll take them on, give them a few spins, mix them up with our personal struggle and psychodrama, and throw them back in your face in caricature form. I remember all the guys who turned up in the clubs with the big gold chains, giant high-tops, and elaborate trucker hats. Well, as the equivalent of the urban gay, we now get the gay bro.

I was fortunate enough that the whole urban phenomenon passed me by. I didn't get it. I wasn't attracted to it. I used to see those kids, who were really, really popular, by the way, and think—well, what difference does it make if you're wearing a thick gold chain around your neck and have a smoking gun tattooed on you? You're an insecure gay guy, no different from me, and you're fronting like crazy. It's a Halloween costume.

No good is going to come from pursuing a relationship with a gay bro. Do you think a gay bro is ready to hold you in his big arms, lie in bed with you at night, look into your eyes, and tell you that he loves you? I do not.

In the three months that I've lived in America, despite all my cheerlessness and self-imposed isolation, I have found the time to become obsessed with the bro phenomenon and attempt to take it on myself.

Anyway, this is not about me. This is about bros. How can I find them? How do you identify them in the street, on the beach, in the gay bar where a friend dragged them—honestly, they'd rather be at a sports bar drinking Bud Light—and how do you take them home and have emotionless, guilty-yet-passionate sex with them before they pass out next to you with their arm squashing your chest while you lie awake on your back staring at the ceiling? (Bros don't lose any sleep.)

Being a bro is an all-encompassing endeavor that requires concentrated efforts combining different aspects like their mentality, their behavior, and their look.

How to Be a Bro

1. First of all mentally, they kinda have to play a little dumb. Bros may come with a wide range of intelligence, but the smarter ones can't let you know that. It just takes away from their swag. Of course, bros are not allowed to read anything, so throw away your books. They just turn them off. A very quick way to come across as a bro is to misspell everything. Key words to spell wrong are the present participle forms of every verb. For example: they can never type "just chilling." It always has to be "just chillen." "Drinking" is "drinken," "golfing" is "golfen," etc. Spelling things wrong adds to the perceived insolence that's a key aspect of the bro persona. Of course the bro doesn't care about you. He doesn't even care enough to use the autocorrect suggestion. You can take it or leave it. (I'll take it.)

   No one can ever convince me that when I receive a text message that describes something as "amaxing," the bro did this by accident. Or that his iPhone didn't suggest "amazing" instead. It's just that the bro chose it this way, as part of his act. Sometimes he will also text you with ridiculous typos, which again, should not be happening in the day and age of autocorrect, but here we are and they do. When you receive a text that includes the words "maYbe" or "headingt to th game," you know that he ignored the autocorrect suggestion. The message the bro is sending you is that he doesn't have the time for this shit. He's heading to the game. You'll figure it out.

2. Second, bros have a very particular way of speaking to one another, as well as other people. All communication should start with "sup" or "whaddup" and everyone should be addressed with "bro," "bruh," "brah" (both are acceptable), "boss," "dawg," or even the classic "dude." They can call their gym buddies "dude," but they can also call their mother "dude." It's one and the same.

3. Bros drink. A lot. Watery American beer, mainly, but also bourbon, shots, and wine when they want to be more sophisticated at a dinner party (before asking the host if there's any beer, actually, or failing that, bourbon). If they're tailgating, which combines their two main raisons d'être—sports and drinking—they'll basically drink anything and everything that will get them the most paralytic the quickest.

4. Music choices include EDM and country. That's it. Bros have to attend Coachella, of course, which is unofficially known as Hipster Bro Christmas, but they don't have to watch any of the alternative bands. They can just spend three days in Sahara, the DJ tent, where they will drink, hook up, intimidate other festival goers, and perform the trademark bro dance of extending their right arm high above their head with an open palm facing down and moving it to the beat while they're standing still. Oh, they may also jump up and down briefly when their pills kick in. They also tend to go to Stagecoach, obviously. Stagecoach is a country music festival that takes place in the same venue as Coachella, a week

later, and it single-handedly stands for everything I both despise and lust over when it comes to American bros.

5. Posing. When they're having their picture taken, the primary goal is to come across as a badass. It is imperative that they do one of the following: (a) stick their tongue out in a silly/insolent way (the right expression comes with time and practice), (b) wink, and (c) give the camera the finger. I've never seen a bro do all three together and I think it may be possible in Florida, exclusively.

6. Finally, the look. Bros' whole look is pretending not to have one. They're not like the other gays who worry about clothes, fashion, looks, and trends. They're too straight actin for that. Bros wear what makes them feel comfortable. This is, naturally, bullshit. Bros care about their look *a lot*. There is no other scientific explanation as to why all of them, bro after bro, make the same clothing/accessory choices. There is no other reason why they rest their sunglasses on the back of their neck, instead of the top of their head. It's impractical and they might lose them. But they still do it, because at some point they saw another bro wearing them that way, and this bro didn't look like he cared about his sunglasses, so now neither do they.

Other key fashion choices are: bandannas, lanyards to carry their keys, anything with a USA flag print, hoodies, socks pulled up high at the gym, wearing their

T-shirt inside out because they happened to put it on that way and don't care enough to change it, anything from Under Armour, those compression shorts that you wear underneath your shorts at the gym when you play sports, boat shoes with board shorts, boat shoes with white socks, Nike, flannel shirts when they're in a gay club because they don't need to show off their muscles, and the ultimate bro accessory—the backward baseball cap.

The backward baseball cap is the one, conclusive, unquestionable statement to the world that this bro may be gay, but he's also masc musc nonscene. These people are not taken seriously as bros unless they wear a backward hat at least 80 percent of the time. For the other 20 percent, they turn it forward. The choice of baseball cap that they make is very wide. They do find it safer to stick to the classics though: their college team, their hometown team, the team of a city they've never been to but like the colors of, any fucking team will do. They can mix it up with some Nike or Under Armour, occasionally. They don't wear one of those big caps with the gay slogans though, as their backward baseball cap must never be humorous or camp. Those caps are exactly the opposite of what they're trying to do. Bros wear their baseball cap everywhere. There are literally no fucking limits. They can wear it in the gym and sweat through it like a motherfucker (but they'll look masculine), they can wear it to the gay bars (and they'll look nonscene and everyone will want to fuck them), and they can even wear it in the evening at semiformal dinners with a long-sleeved, button-down shirt (and they'll look fratty, which is something they want).

That's it. It's quite easy for most people to follow these rules and become a bro. If someone does, I will probably want him. If someone already knows me and I don't currently want him, he can try putting on a backward baseball cap. I will probably change my mind immediately.

JUNE

10

Heartbreak is really funny to anyone who's not suffering it. It comes with all sorts of overreaction and volatile behavior. Imagine the heartbreak caused by your partner leaving you for someone else. You will feel bitter, you will feel wronged, and you will feel vengeful. That's bound to cause you to be a little irrational. You'll want everyone to know what happened to you and that it wasn't your fault. And if you're not the person who's feeling this way, if you're just an outsider observing, this will all be quite hilarious. Do I think that for the end of any relationship only one person is to blame? I don't. And was I completely surprised when Brett walked out on me after four years together and started dating someone else without even flinching? Was I under the impression that everything was going so perfectly between us and when it ended the way it did, was I completely blindsided? Again, no. In retrospect I get the feeling that Brett wanted out of our relationship for quite a while. We had taken some breaks but always ended up together again. But this time, having found someone new, Brett had no reason to come back. I get it. But being aware of these things is not making this any easier.

Being in LA is also not making this any easier. I'm surrounded by people who I don't know very well and although I tried their approach, to go out in full force and start living my life again, I'm just not ready. I need to be near people that I know a little better and I need to take a step back. The only friend on this whole continent that I've known for a long time and is completely outside this circle is my friend Willa, who went to Uni in London, where we met, before moving back to the U.S. a few years later. She lives in San Francisco with her husband. They've offered to put me up for as long as I need to figure out what I want to do next. In the first weekend of June, I pack the few things that I have, leave my short-let apartment in WeHo, and drive north.

There's nothing to say about the first couple of weeks. I don't eat, I don't sleep, I don't work, I don't listen to music or watch TV or read. I just wait. I also don't want to have anything to do with any guy who goes out and is part of the scene because, possibly as some sort of coping mechanism inspired by my own gay insecurities and self-loathing, I'm putting a lot of the blame for what happened on this. The gay lifestyle: going out, sleeping around, getting drunk, taking drugs, the bars and clubs and parties. Like nonscene gays or even straight people have never been cheated on and dumped before. So I guess I'm happily entertaining my delusions that I will eventually find contentment if I stay isolated in this house long enough.

Apart from being inactive and waiting, I continue to seek out updates of what's going on in London with Brett and his now fiancé. This is not something I can stop myself from doing. And the more I find out, the crazier I get. It really seems that they are now engaged. This is insane.

How is it possible that someone can have a boyfriend for four years, then suddenly they make plans to get married to another guy three months later and nobody questions this? And I ask that question via Facebook Messenger to my friend Sean in London, who's bitter too, I guess and Sean says:

"Because we're gay. This is expected. So you're at a dinner party, then three people disappear from the table and the next thing you know is that they're all fucking in the bathroom. You think that anyone will raise an eyebrow at some London queen changing boyfriends all of a sudden?"

And this makes perfect sense, of course.

11

On Wednesday I'm chatting on Facebook with my friend Todd who is American but lives in Australia, which is very convenient for me, as it gives me somebody to talk to when America has gone to bed and Europe hasn't woken up yet. It may be obvious to add at this point that I have currently run out of sleeping pills. After Australia I start talking to Central Europe, after that Western Europe, after that the East Coast of America, and by the time I catch up with my own time zone on the West Coast I haven't slept for three days, but at least I have been social.

Todd has a bad history of being attracted to terrible, terrible people who treat him like shit, but he just can't help it. He wants it really bad. These terrible, terrible people exhibit all sorts of objectionable behavior, like cheating on him behind his back, being hookers behind his back, being drug addicts both in front of and behind his back, etc. Naturally Todd usually finds his boyfriends at circuit parties, like the rest of us. Saying that, Todd is actually a nice person and would deserve to be with somebody that treats him well, but he's also in this weird predicament where he's hormonally imbalanced and exclusively attracted to people on steroids who went to Mykonos last August, so I don't know what to tell him, really.

So, on this Wednesday Todd messages me:

"Konrad! I watched the video on Instagram of you giving yourself a haircut with your shirt off. Who are you trying to impress?"

"Just trying to feel sexually desirable, to be honest. (Via reducing myself and prostituting my image)"

"Ooh, my ex is a hooker. I can get you tips"

"No, thanks. I have enough bad exes now. Don't need other people's too"

"Interesting. Also my ex still asks me for money, so I haven't done very well"

"He can't be a very good hooker then. In any case, you definitely win"

"I don't want to win"

"One can win at losing. Not that I think you're a loser. Just attracted to the wrong men"

"Well, we have clearly established that. But I don't think that's going to change anytime soon"

"You might bump into a good one by accident though?"

"I don't think that I will. Regardless, I will spend the next forty years looking. Over and over and over again"

"Same"

Then Todd has to go to the gym, so I move on to my next time zone.

12

I've been in San Francisco for about a month, although sometimes it feels much longer and sometimes it feels like I got here yesterday; it's kinda hard to keep track of time when you're shut off in a room crushing and snorting sedatives, sleeping pills, and ketamine, typing furiously in your journal and monitoring the online profiles of your ex and his new boyfriend and that's *all* you are doing. In this month I've not spoken to any real-life people apart from Willa and her husband and I'm told that this isn't healthy, apparently, so I must go out and socialize. Willa puts me in touch with the only two other gay people she knows in the city, and we all know what a disaster it is when straight people put gay people together, but I message Graeme and Gene anyway and make plans to meet up. Graeme and Gene are a couple in their midforties. Willa has briefed them that I am currently a train wreck and they are nice and accommodating and willing to do whatever I want to do this evening. But I don't know what I want to do, so they suggest we hit the town.

We meet up and have dinner and then go to this club, which starts at 10:00 P.M. We have no drugs apart from some weed. Have you ever gone clubbing stoned? Don't.

The club is boring. Nobody's passing out in the corner and no circuit queens have even bothered to turn up, although there might be none in San Francisco, I don't know. Then a guy that I'm very interested in gets there with three other guys that I'm really not into. The guy that I like is tall and has wide shoulders and the mopish wavy hair of a frat bully, not unlike an early-day Brandon from Sean Cody. A friend of Graeme and Gene's knows the four of them and takes me over to introduce me. Then he immediately walks away and I'm left with Brandon Sean Cody and his friends. All four people in my new group are very friendly, although their exact level of friendliness is inversely proportional to how attractive they are. I'm not very clever, but I do think this is how most humans work.

After a few minutes I leave my new friends and go back to my old friends, because sometimes I like to pretend that I have good manners. Also so I can find out who's going out with whom in the group of four, because their interactions are confusing me.

"Please tell me that the tall guy over there is single," I ask.

"The pretty one? Yes, he is. The other three are in a three-way relationship. But he's single."

Of course they are. Regardless, this is satisfactory.

Then Graeme and Gene decide to leave and go home because they are in their forties and don't need this anymore and I decide to stay because at some point, somewhere, in my midtwenties, I lost all sense of what's wrong and what's right.

So I go and join my new friends, who are now on the dance floor with their shirts off in the middle of a whole big group of other people like the ones I have supposedly been trying to get away from. I spend the next seven hours with them, and then I go home, alone.

13

I started off by feeling sorry for every poor soul who would see me in the gym, or on Grindr, or on Scruff, or on Adam4Adam, or on RealJock, or on OkCupid, or on Big Muscle (I'm covering all the bases) and decide to approach me. I kinda thought, there's no way that I'm not going to fuck over anyone that I meet in the next six months, at least. Then I went on a couple of actual dates and realized that I'm overestimating my importance once again. I can't do that to all these people. They're already fucked up. I'm not bringing anything new.

The avenues through which I'm supposed to meet all these men that I've typed above are not accidental. What are my strengths as a single, gay man? What do I have to offer? I have a decent body that photographs well and an overactive mind. But I'm socially awkward and don't do any activities and don't interact well and get tired of the outdoors very quickly.

Where does that leave me? Not in a great place. Bars are out. Social gatherings are out. Dinner parties are out. Networking events are out. Gay camping trips that include rafting are out (that's a thing, I'm not making this up). So what's left? The gym and online.

In the gym you don't have to say anything, you just have to work out and make studied eye contact (or not make eye contact at all) and someone will come up and talk to you eventually, if they like your triceps. Especially in America. Oh America. How do they bring you up like that? So forward, upbeat, and self-assured? I'm not really complaining. It's just that when you come talk to me, I'm a little bit scared.

Online you can throw some shirtless pictures on and hope for the best. Then when people message you and start a conversation, you can use your words. I can handle online conversations well. It's in real life where I falter.

All this makes for very promising online encounters and brief, awkward gym conversations. Then we meet for a date and actually have to spend real time with each other. And that's where the fun starts.

14

The unfortunate thing for the straight-acting, nonscene Berkeley or Stanford graduate bros currently living in the suburbs (or Palo Alto) who message me on any of the apps that I'm on is that they don't realize that somebody who has six to eight visible abdominal muscles at any given point has not led a normal, balanced life so far and, more importantly, is not mentally stable. Still, they're so oblivious that they think I got those by participating in sports with my college buddies, or playing catch with extended family members at Sunday afternoon picnics in our grandparents' backyards, dressed in chinos and pastels, dirty blond fringes flopping in the wind. Admittedly, the fact that I wear chinos and pastels in all my clothed pictures must also add to the confusion.

Overall the compatibility between fallen circuit queens trying to escape the scene and nonscene upmarket bros is very, very low. Not only are these nonscene bros terrified of me, but I'm also appalled by them, because, you know, you're a grown man living in a liberal area, get over yourself.

On Friday evening last week, I get a text message from a nonscene bro in Palo Alto that I gave my number to on Adam4Adam maybe a couple of weeks ago. I'm going to call him John, because, well, it doesn't really matter. I don't know why John decided to message me now, because I don't follow any sports so I don't know what season just finished to empty his weekends, but in any case, this is a conversation that goes like this:

John: What are you plans tonight/tmrw?

Me: Tonight I'm tired at home falling asleep. Tomorrow I have zero plans

John: K I'll be working tmrw, would u be able to come down to pa?

Me: I could come down

John: Grab a drink?

Me: Sure thing

John: Cool cool, what's ur drink/smoke of choice?

Me: Actually, I'll drink anything

John: Haha nice, smoke?

Me: What are you talking about? Weed? Yeah maybe

John: Just cigs

Me: No, I don't smoke cigarettes at all. You must think I'm very boring

John: Haha np. You wouldn't change ur mind on any of those, would ya?

Me: You want me to drive down to Palo Alto, so we can smoke cigarettes together?

John: Yeah can I corrupt you?

Me: I fear I'm a lot more corrupted than you think, John

John: Haha what do u mean?

Me: Never mind. So what are we going to do?

John: Haha u tell me

Me: Make out? Fuck? I don't know. I'm just throwing
things out there. I'm sure even Palo Alto straight
bros like to do these things from time to time

John: Haha I wanna see u be corrupted

I'm not sure if this is suburban code for getting double-penetrated and I'm not prepared for that, so I ask:

Me: How?

John: Smoke?

Me: Is that all?

John: We'll go from there, if ur down?

Me: Is smoking a big thing for you?

John: Ha nah. Just a turn-on.

Me: I'm not leaving the house for any less than snorting
a line of coke off your cock

Then John doesn't reply. Then I go to bed. Then it's nine
thirty Saturday evening and I text John again:

Me: "Hey, I just got here, where do you want to meet?

Then John doesn't reply again.

15

On Sunday evening I convince myself that I will have the first good night's sleep since January by starting to take inadvisable combinations of sedatives and sleeping pills early on, therefore building a gradual state of tranquility, hopefully slumber, that will take me through to the next morning. This plan is in contrast to my usual nonchalant method of trying to go without, then finding myself wide awake at 4:00 A.M. with a throbbing pain in my temples, running through the events of the last couple of months. So at 9:00 P.M., I take 2 mg of Xanax, followed by another 2 mg at 10:00 P.M., followed by 5 mg of Ambien at 11:00 P.M. Around midnight I start Ambien-posting on Twitter, until I suddenly pass out. At 2:30 A.M., I wake up. I stay awake for an hour, trying to figure out how it's possible to have an increased heart rate and a void feeling where my heart used to be at the same time.

Eventually I crush and snort 2 mg of Xanax and 3.25 mg of Zopiclone (that's half a pill) because it works faster than just swallowing them. At 5:00 A.M., I wake up again and take half an Ambien (swallowed) and the other half of the Zopiclone that's left from earlier (snorted). At 6:45 A.M. I wake up again, go to the bathroom, take a mirror selfie demonstrating my abs looking particularly violent, because all these pills dehydrate the hell out of me, and post it on Instagram. I wait until it's had at least 350 likes before feeling like I'm worth something as a human being. This feeling lasts about two minutes, until somebody that I don't know leaves a snippy comment about me being self-absorbed. Then I turn my phone off and go back to sleep.

I wake up at 10:30 A.M. with a tolerable headache and down 2.5 liters of water before checking Facebook, Instagram, Snapchat, and Grindr. On Facebook there is universal uproar from a bunch of gay men who've spent their weekend sucking dick in club toilets and are now passing judgment on how trashy Miley Cyrus is, based on her performance at the VMAs.

Late in the afternoon, I make my way to the gym. The gym might as well be empty apart from one guy. He's tall, in his midtwenties, and on tons of anabolic steroids (good ones). He also seems to be on some sort of amphetamine or another, which I'm sure he refers to as his "preworkout." Whatever. He's high. He's literally racing around the gym, eyes darting around maniacally, lifting weights in a state of frenzy. I recognize him as somebody I spoke to on Grindr before. Soon enough, I have the honor and the privilege for his crazy eyes to fall upon me in real life too. From the moment he clocks me I become his new obsession.

His first course of action is to come stand behind me and lift his shirt up to check his abdominal muscles in the mirror. I am the person that I am, so that kinda works for me.

His second course of action is to sit on the bench next to me and pretend that he's working out there. He turns to me and mouths something that I don't hear, as I've got headphones on. I remove them and say:

"Hi, yes, we spoke on Grindr earlier, didn't we?"

This is not what he has just said. He has just said that he likes the tattoos on my arms. He proceeds to lift his shirt up again and show me his chest, sorry, "a tattoo on his chest," which is even worse than the ones I have.

"That's really cool," I say.

"Thanks, man. I remember talking on the app, by the way. What's your name again?"

"Konrad."

"Ah yeah that's right. And you're from . . ."

He asks that because he can hear I have an accent. "Germany," I say.

"Yeah yeah I remember."

There is no way he remembers, as I never told him before.

"We should get a drink sometime. Let me get your number," he says.

"All right."

"Come with, I've left my phone in my locker."

I walk with him to the changing room and put my number in his phone. While I'm doing that, he points at my shirt, which randomly has "1987" on it, and says:

"Dude, that's incredible, that's the year I was born. You

know, we've got similar tattoos . . . your shirt shows my birth year . . . you've got me all over you. Well, hopefully."

He runs his fingers across the writing on my chest, outlining each number, I get a semi, and then I leave.

We go on a date a couple of days later. The best part of the date is when we discuss Germany and he asks, "They speak German over there, right, or Latin?"

The second best part of the date is when I tell him halfway through dinner that we have absolutely nothing in common, to which he seems to take offense, because you know, we have to sit there and pretend that we're soul mates and we're going to spend the rest of our lives together when all we want to do is fuck tonight and never see each other again.

After dinner I disregard the fact that he's a complete moron and he appears to disregard the fact that I've been nothing but a dick to him, and we go back to his place together. He takes his clothes off and I stand there in awe for a bit, because his body is insane. I ask whether everyone reacts the same way when they see him naked for the first time, and he says, "Pretty much." Then we start making out. Then we're both naked in bed. Then I realize that this is actually the first time that I'm about to have sex with someone since my breakup. And I start to cry. Or rather, I lose my hard-on and I start to cry. The insanely hot guy doesn't understand what's happening exactly, so I sit there for the next ten minutes sobbing and give him a brief outline of my heartbreak, which I'm 100 percent sure is not how he wanted to be spending his Wednesday evening, and then I grab my clothes and leave.

On Wednesday morning I go see my new doctor here in

San Francisco and ask for a PrEP prescription, because I guess it's time to come to terms with the fact that I am definitely single, I will be going on dates, and at some point in the near future I might even stop breaking down in tears in front of them when we get naked and actually start having sex. So this is as good a time as any.

16

On this empty Wednesday morning I have nothing to do and no one to account to. I could be doing absolutely anything with my free time, anywhere on this planet, so I sit here at my desk and scan my recommended friends tab on Facebook, looking for someone to flirt with. I scroll through thumbnail profile pictures of young gay men scattered around the country and click to send a friend request to anyone who stands out. People can stand out by being male, under forty-five, and having worked out at least three times in the last week. Consequently, eight out of ten people on average in my recommended friends stand out. Online desperation is a game of numbers, apparently, and soon enough a few of these prospects start accepting me, and just like that we are now in each other's lives.

I click into the profile of a thick-necked Neanderthal called Aaron Wellinger who resides in Little Rock, wherever that is, and see that his last post is from yesterday evening when he uploaded a picture of himself standing in a gym with his shirt off flexing his muscles with the tagline "Why not." He looks hot as fuck. I google Little Rock to find out where it is and message him:

"Hey man, hows life in Arkansas"

He writes back:

"Hey [smiley emoji]. Not too bad. Cloudy today. How are you"

"I'm good. We're having pretty good weather here in LA. I like your pictures"

"I like yours too"

Then I don't write for a bit because someone buzzes me from downstairs and I have to go pick up a delivery and when I come back upstairs I check my messages and Aaron has written:

"You message me and immediately disappear? Typical [winking emoji with tongue sticking out]"

I write back:

"Why do we have to fight all the time? Smh"

Then Aaron decides to continue the conversation by sending four almost identical shirtless pictures of him looking into a mirror, with the only variation being what he's wearing from the waist down. Also, on his head. In one picture he's wearing a pair of black sweat shorts. In the second picture he's wearing just a white towel. In the third picture he's not wearing anything, but his dick is obscured by a strategically positioned bathroom sink. In the fourth picture he's wearing a white towel again, but this time he's also wearing a green baseball cap with a bill that's way too curved, but it will have to do.

In response to those, I send him a picture in my underwear, standing in my bedroom looking very angrily into the camera. He then replies with two emojis: a smiley face with two hearts instead of eyes, and a wedding ring. Then he also sends me his number.

We spend the next hour or so talking sexual positions and exchanging dick and ass pictures. Then suddenly, Aaron takes it to the next level and sends me a video, quite unprompted. The video starts with a shot of a bed in an empty room. I understand this is his bedroom. There is a framed illustration of the Little Rock skyline on the wall above his bed, and I only know this because it also includes the words LITTLE ROCK printed on it. I can also see a vintage Arkansas RiverBlades poster and a couple of whiskey-related framed prints. Then Aaron steps into the frame naked, ass first, facing away from the camera. He walks up to the bed and takes a position on it on all fours. He spends the next twenty seconds or so on his knees curving his lower back up and down and quietly moaning as though he's being fucked by someone invisible. When this is over, he gets up, still facing away so you never get to see his face, walks back closer to the camera, gives a little wave, then a victory sign, and turns it off.

I give him the enthusiastic response he is looking for and a picture of my erect dick. He messages and says that "he wants this to belong to him." I tell him that "the same applies to his ass; mine." He says, "I'm yours baby."

Then I don't message anymore because I think that the conversation has come to a natural end for now, but an hour later he writes, "ouch." I ask him what's wrong and he complains that I disappeared right after he told me that he wants to be property of Konrad Platt. I apologize and say that I want to meet up. He asks me when it's good, and he'll fly to me whenever I want. He adds that he needs to come visit soon, because he doesn't like the idea of me being with other dudes now that we've met.

We stop talking again and an hour later he sends a second video. The video opens with a close-up shot of a dildo, which I believe is positioned on some low piece of furniture in his bedroom. He walks into the frame again in the same manner as the first video, looking away, and proceeds to crouch down, spread his ass open and sit on the dildo. He fucks himself for a bit that way before standing up and giving his signature wave and victory sign, and then the video ends. I ask him why he's doing this to me and add that I want him so bad. He says, "We have to meet ASAP."

Then I go to the gym. An hour later he starts texting me again. He says that he wants me to be serious when I talk about us. That he likes it when I say that I want his butt to be only mine. And that he wants me. I say that I want him too. Then the conversation goes a bit like this.

Aaron: I have free flights with miles that are earmarked
        to come see you.
Me: Let's do it.

Then half an hour later:

Aaron: So.
Me: So?
Aaron: Never mind. Good night.
Me: Wow
Aaron: Well
Me: Well what?

Aaron: Nothing

Me: Wow again

Aaron: True

Me: I'm not sure what's going on in this conversation, but I don't believe it's following any of the social norms I've ever come across before.

Aaron: Well I'm drunk. You're not being sweet or attentive. So there we are.

Me: I'm sorry

The next morning he sends me a text at seven with a sad face emoji. I happen to be awake and reply:

Me: Where were you last night?

Aaron: At a bar

Me: What was happening there?

Aaron: Nothing. Was just thirsty.

Me: What do you think of our conversation last night?

Aaron: Can we just not discuss it and pretend it didn't happen please

Me: Sure

Aaron: Thanks bae

Aaron: You mad

Me: Yes. I'm very mad. You are not allowed to drink anymore.

Aaron: Ha. Good luck. So I want more attention from you. Big deal

Me: I mean

Aaron: Be nice. Isn't a hangover punishment enough?

Then I fall back asleep and wake up at 10:00 A.M. He texts me around 11:00 A.M. with a frowning emoji. I text back with an emoji with a straight line for a mouth.

Aaron: You my bae

Me: You are mine forever. You are my love

Aaron: That's the kind of stuff I want you to be serious about

Me: But Aaron. Let me level with you. We have exchanged, like, ten messages. We have only spoken for a day. I do think you're incredibly sexy. And you also seem nice, etc. But we don't know each other yet. And I don't understand how we can go from "meeting" online one day to saying these things to each other the next. It's odd. Even if the promise is there, I don't believe these things when you say them and I don't want to say them back because they are hollow and not true. I just don't understand what you want us to do right now. And that's everything.

Aaron: It's cool. Just don't message me anymore though. Take care dude.

Then I block his number, block him on Facebook, and go to bed.

17

On Friday I wake up just before eight and I decide that this is a good time to get up, because this is a time that somebody who might actually have somewhere to be might also get up and start their day. The arrangement of having a more or less part-time job I can do from home on my own time is really working out for me.

I remember watching a German sitcom when I was very young, maybe twelve or thirteen, and this sitcom was about some very rich heiress who owned a bunch of factories or whatever and she never had to go to work, and there was this financial adviser guy she employed and he would sometimes come to see her at ten or eleven in the morning and he would wake her up, which always angered her, because her big thing, her life philosophy, was that she just wants to have one luxury in life and nothing else: she wants to wake up whenever she feels like waking up, naturally, without anyone, alarm clock or other human being, interrupting her sleep. Because she thought that when you're asleep your soul leaves your body or something, and when you get abruptly awakened, your soul gets rushed into your body forcefully instead of returning peacefully, quietly, in its own time, and that's really destructive for you as a person. That was the sitcom's big joke, anyway. That she was so spoiled that she didn't have anywhere to be, nothing to interrupt her sleep for. And when I watched that it really bugged me. I mean it must have really bugged me a lot, I still remember it now twenty years later, because I thought, Oh my god, who is she? How can she possibly think like that? That's not just one luxury, that's just an impossible luxury, because it means you never have to go to work, you never have to go to school (I was twelve), you don't have any responsibilities or commitments to anyone. So in my head, this freedom of time, this endless, uninterrupted sleep was the impossible luxury, the ultimate sign of achievement and happiness, something so completely unattainable and unrealistic that it was used as a comedic device in this low-budget German sitcom in 1992.

Now I wake up every day whenever I want without an alarm clock and I'm still really not quite sure where my soul is left wandering. Surely I would be able to feel it if it were part of me somehow, so I guess whoever wrote that German sitcom in 1992 was wrong: waking up at your leisure and having nowhere to go, no responsibilities or commitments to anyone, will not, by default, make you happy.

I have breakfast and think about leaving the house. Then I don't see a reason to leave the house, so I stay in.

A couple of hours pass and Willa asks me to meet her for lunch at this restaurant near her office, so I wear a button-down shirt and chinos instead of a T-shirt and shorts even though it's rather warm and sunny, because Willa will be wearing her work clothes and I don't want to show up and embarrass her.

After lunch Willa goes back to work and I go back home, because I'm trying this new thing where I'm attempting to find some self-worth outside what my body looks like, so I've reduced my gym-going to only five days a week, and I stay there until 7:00 P.M. talking to people via text or online and watching *30 Rock* from the beginning and I don't give up even when it becomes stale.

Willa then texts me and says that she's going to the cinema to watch a movie with Paul and asks if I want to join them, so we text back and forth for about an hour trying to arrange this, then I decide that it's too much effort to go back all the way over there and I leave the house to go get some food at Whole Foods instead.

At Whole Foods I see a gentleman that I find very attractive, who's not just age appropriate (30+) but also doing a full-on grocery shop on a Friday night at eight, which means that he's perfect and ready to settle down. He is muscular and has tattoos, so I'm making the initial assumption that he's gay. Then I look at him for a few seconds and he catches my eye, then I walk away and pick up some food and walk toward the checkout and bump into him again on the way and we look at each other again, but perhaps only because I'm forcing it, and then I get to the checkout and pay for my teriyaki chicken bowl. I decide to take the long way out of the store so that I can see him a third time, and I see him a third time and we look at each other again, then he raises his arm and mouths something in my direction, which sends some very brief shock waves through my stomach and heart, until I realize that he's actually trying to talk to somebody behind me—the person that he's here with—but I don't turn around to see if the person is male or female, gay or straight, age appropriate or not, and I just exit the store quickly, looking intensely at the ground.

When I get home, I eat my dinner and decide to go back to the gym.

18

On Thursday morning it's raining and I'm sitting at home watching YouTube videos of pop songs that I like but I'm too embarrassed to own and play on my iTunes, so I stream online instead. A message pops up on my Facebook from a guy called Lloyd Ellis, whom I'm not friends with and know nothing about. Lloyd's profile picture is a selfie taken in his car. He is driving, but he's not wearing a shirt, nor is he wearing a seat belt. He looks like he's in his early thirties and he is unfeasibly handsome. In fact, he is so handsome that there must be something seriously wrong with him mentally, emotionally, or in any other possible covert way for him to be messaging random men on Facebook on a Thursday morning trying to make conversation with them. If there were nothing wrong underneath the surface with a guy who has that face, build, and overall demeanor, on a Thursday morning he would be making a speech at the World Economic Forum, or he would be addressing his alma mater as a graduation speaker before catching a flight to go back home and spend the evening with his slightly less handsome, equally high-achieving husband in their Chelsea loft. He is that superhumanly attractive. Doors don't just open up for him, doors fall off their hinges, come to life, and set themselves on fire to let him through. He is Apollo, he is the ruler of Valhalla, he is an angel and a god.

Then again, it is the beginning of August and maybe he did address both the World Economic Forum and Harvard earlier in the year and I am, perhaps, being unfair. Then I click on his profile and see that he lives in Buffalo, New York, and the only education information provided goes up to a local college, but none of these red flags deter me from messaging him back, because now I have seen his traps and it's too late for me.

His message reads: "How's it going out in Cali?"

Clicking into the conversation I see that he had also messaged me unprompted a few months ago, very soon after I moved to the U.S., to ask, "How's LA?" but I guess I missed seeing that one back then, plus I wasn't really in the mood to talk to strangers at the time, but right now it's all I do, so I write back and we continue talking and assessing each other as potential prospects.

Me: It's going . . . OK. Getting used to it still, moved here recently

Lloyd: Where did u move from? That's awesome! Want to get out there myself.

Me: Moved from London. So quite a big change.

Lloyd: Very cool! Well good luck, by the looks of it you won't need it

Me: I don't know . . . everyone needs a bit of luck.

At this point he sends a friend request, which I accept, and then go and review his profile a bit more. We have a few friends in common who live in LA. One of them is Markus, the guy that Anthony is living with, and two others are Daniel and Rus, from the threeway relationship with X.

Me: So you've never lived out here? You have quite a few
  friends in California though?
Lloyd: I haven't though hopefully someday soon. I have
  always wanted to live in southern California. I've
  made a few friends there. How are you liking it
  so far?
Me: Well, I first moved to LA but I only stayed there for
  a couple months and I'm now living in San Francisco. I don't know where I want to be long-term.
Lloyd: I'm in Buffalo. I grew up here but I travel a lot,
  love traveling. I love LA and every time I go I forget
  how good-looking and gay that city is which is always
  fun but want a city with more substance. It KILLS
  being in Buffalo now though.

Then I think, oh my god, finally a guy who looks like that but also has some real substance and then I ask him what he does for work.

Lloyd: I work in hospitality consulting and can transfer
  anywhere in the country but to be honest I hate it
  and when I get there I'm leaving the consulting
  world.

I don't know exactly what that means but it sounds really great to me right now, especially assessed alongside his jawline and the size of his biceps, so I write back something encouraging and then he asks me if I'm single and I say yes and then he writes back that he's dancing around the room at this news and then we leave it there for a bit and I go to the gym.

Later in the evening, he messages me again, because we are now fully preoccupied with each other, I guess, and the conversation goes like this.

Lloyd: How come you moved all the way from London to Cali?

The fact that he keeps referring to California as Cali is starting to bug me, because even I, having lived here for only a few months, know that you're not supposed to do that, but I suppose he doesn't know any better, and I write back.

Me: Well, I don't want to get into the details, but I was in a long-term relationship in London and it ended by him starting something behind my back with someone else, and I didn't want to be in the same city as them anymore, so I felt like moving as far away as possible. And my dad lives in CA, so I thought I'd try it out over here for a while.

Lloyd: I feel sick reading that. That's why I can't live in West Hollywood. It's just a different mind-set when it comes to relationships. So many of those hot "glamorous" gays in the big cities like LA and London are just smoke and mirrors. They wear a good suit to project wealth, drive a nice car, and they chase the next hot guy but after they cum what is left? Nothing.

Me: Yeah, I don't know. What's most hurtful is that it all happened without me knowing anything. If some-one feels like the love is gone and the relationship needs to end, he needs to be up front about it.

Lloyd: The cheating lying thing is the line I draw. You really think you should have to check up on your bf? Trust is crucial. And when that's gone it becomes so exhausting. I've been there.

I like him a little bit more, and then he says that he has to go to bed, because it is three hours ahead over there after all, and then I see that the rain has stopped for the first time today, so I take my iPod and go outside for a walk.

Halfway through New Order's *Technique,* I get a FaceTime call from Anthony in LA and Anthony knows that I don't talk on the phone and I've told him it's going to have to be an emergency if he calls me again, so this could possibly be an emergency or he may just be high and have forgotten again, but I answer either way.

Anthony is not exactly lucid and he launches into a story about having just been arrested. I guess that's entertaining enough so I listen to it and the story goes that he just left a wedding with Markus and Markus needed to pee really badly, so before starting to drive he stepped behind his car and started peeing on the street and Anthony thought that maybe he'd pee as well while he was waiting, so he walked two cars down and took his dick out and before he had the chance to pee, a police car pulled up and shone lights on them and yelled at them and handcuffed them, and Anthony feels this was completely unfair as he hadn't even started peeing yet, but now he has a court date where he has to show up and be faced with one day in jail or a $2,500 fine or community service and he also gets a criminal record, but at least he was lucky enough that there wasn't a school in the area, because he would have also been registered as a sex offender if there was.

Then I also go to bed.

19

On Wednesday afternoon I'm at the gym and see the really forward hot guy I disastrously hooked up with a few weeks ago who didn't know whether they speak German or Latin in Germany, and I want to flirt with him again and I want to try hooking up with him again to prove something to myself, but he's well and truly done with me and he won't even catch my eye or say hi to me, and who can blame him really?

When I go home I start talking to Lloyd online again like we have been doing almost every day since those first messages we exchanged three weeks ago. A lot of these conversations have now even been on Skype, we're not just typing stuff. This is a full-blown made-up long-distance love affair.

Today I really want to find out exactly how he knows the people he knows in LA, because I investigated on Facebook very thoroughly and found some pictures of him actually hanging out with Daniel, Rus, and X. Well, the actor doesn't appear in the pictures because he doesn't appear in any Facebook pictures, but there are pictures of Lloyd hanging out with the other two.

I can tell this is a very sensitive subject and he doesn't want to talk about it, because from what I understand they flew him out there and he had some sort of weekend sexual affair with them, and this goes against the whole image of himself he wants to present to me, where he's wholesome and moral as fuck and disapproves of promiscuity and those "glamorous city gays."

So I ask some very detailed questions and find out that this is exactly what happened two years ago, yes, but he's really regretted it and has moved on as a person and he was really young at the time and he was very naïve and he would never do anything like this again, and if I want to know actually, these people used him and they're really disgusting and he wants to have nothing to do with them anymore.

My initial reaction is, well, you're a thirty-four-year-old man, you're fully aware of what you're doing, but I don't want to antagonize him too much because he's the closest I have to a potential boyfriend right now and I really need to have a boyfriend, no, I simply must have a boyfriend to prove to Brett and everyone else who knows me back in London and now in California that I'm not some kind of loser who gets cheated on and dumped and can't find anyone to date him, so I give up on the interrogation, concede that perhaps he was used and he has learned his lesson and he has moved on now and is a different person, and then we jerk off on camera, cum, and hang up.

Then I start texting Anthony and asking him to ask Markus what he knows about Lloyd, because they're also Facebook friends, and this kind of gossipy backstabbing is right up Anthony's street, so I know that he'll deliver.

"What's there to know? Markus says that he's an opportunistic, freeloading gay."

"And what evidence does Markus have of that, please?"

"Well, he met those guys at some circuit party at Market Days in Chicago a few years back. They took him back to their hotel and fucked him. Then a few months after that they flew him out here, paraded him around, and fucked him a bit more."

"Hmm."

"Oh and then this happened one more time. Everyone in LA knows. Markus says just ask anyone."

"I don't know anyone to ask, so I'm asking you."

"And I'm telling you."

"OK thanks."

"Don't shoot the messenger."

Then I choose to ignore all this because it goes against my current plans to be Lloyd's boyfriend no matter what, get mad at Anthony and Markus for telling me, and unfollow both of them on Instagram for at least half an hour.

20

On Wednesday morning I get on an airplane and fly all the way across the country to go visit Lloyd.

I land at the airport and I'm really exhausted because this is a long trip and there are no direct flights from San Francisco to Buffalo, obviously, and then step outside and wait. Lloyd drives around the airport for half an hour or so and he can't find me and we have several conversations on the phone where I have to reassure him that I'm not catfishing him and I'm not the fat old guy he can see outside arrivals, because this has happened to him before, apparently. As he tells me this I wonder how many people he has created long-distance online relationships with because I'm starting to lose count, and then he finds me.

In real life he is more attractive than any human being has the right to be.

We drive to an Airbnb apartment I've rented for three days because he didn't want me to stay at his house, his roommates are really messy, he said, and he's not on good terms with them and it's just best to have our own space, if I don't mind. I didn't mind, so I paid a few hundred dollars for a horrible place near the water, and in fact I didn't know that Buffalo had a waterfront until I started looking, because I didn't know anything about Buffalo at all.

It's quite late in the evening by the time all this is done. We leave our stuff in the apartment and walk down to the water. Over the course of our communication in the past few weeks, I have found out that what Lloyd meant by "hospitality consulting" was that he works at a hut on the beach renting out kayaks and paddleboards to tourists in the summer months. It's still very unclear what he does in the winter months.

We sit on a blanket and make out a little bit, but it's not very warm and I'm too tired from traveling so we only stay for half an hour and then go home to sleep. The next morning we get up, hang around for a bit, and then he goes to work. I also do some work from home and then walk down to the lake again (I have now been informed that this is a lake and not the ocean, as I may have originally thought) and take a picture sitting on the beach to prove to my 42k Instagram followers that I'm very active, not moping over my ex at all, and moving on with my life. I don't actually say which beach I'm at when I post the picture online, because nobody has ever made anyone jealous by moving on with his life in Buffalo, New York.

On Friday morning Lloyd calls in sick at work and we spend the better part of the day lying in bed together. We also have sex for the first time. It's funny how even the most masculine gay bro drops the pretense when he's in bed with another guy. I guess it's hard to keep playing the straight card when you've got each other's dicks in your mouths. In the afternoon we go to the beach, where I take a picture of him shirtless, just in his board shorts, post it on my Facebook, and tag him, adding the quote "This charming man" from the Smiths' song. Possibly because of the fact that I currently have some goodwill behind me and people are feeling sorry for me, but also because he looks like a Roman god, this quickly becomes the most liked picture I have ever posted. The fact that he has over 2,000 friends on Facebook compared to my paltry 850, therefore catapulting my post to a massive new audience, may also have helped. He posts a picture of me on his own Facebook and adds the tagline "Perfec day" [*sic*].

In the evening we go to a grocery store and buy ingredients for him to make dinner. I've told him that I can't cook to save my life, so now that we are planning our future together, he says that he'll take responsibility for always cooking for us. While he's cooking, I play music on my iPod to entertain us, because I'm the music guy and this is how we'll be doing things from now on.

What he cooks is more or less inedible and the dinner quickly turns into us getting pissed on three bottles of wine and empty stomachs. Even though our interaction has been perfect in the two days that I've been here, his mood noticeably shifts as he gets more and more drunk and he starts becoming irritable and short-tempered with me. Right around this point I stop drinking.

"OK, I wanna ask you this," he says. "How many guys have you been with?"

"Ha. I don't know. I haven't really been counting."

"No. I want you to tell me. How many people have you had sex with?"

"Like, penetrative sex?"

He winces at me in disgust and says yes.

"I really don't know. Many. Why are you asking me this?"

"I just am. Give me a number. You *must* know."

"Um, I really don't, but if you want an estimate I'll say between a hundred and a hundred and fifty. Who cares?"

"That's disgusting, man," he says. "Typical gay man."

"And how many guys have you slept with as a nontypical gay man?" I ask.

"No more than you can count on one hand."

"Well, that is simply not true. You're thirty-four years old, you've been out since you were twenty, and I can already name seven people you've had sex with: the guy you lost your virginity to, the two people you've dated for a year each that you told me about, Rus, Daniel, and X, who flew you to LA, and now me. And I'm pretty sure this can't be the total count in the last fourteen years."

"Yeah it is."

"What does it matter anyway? We're here now, we like each other, and that's all there is to it."

"I bet you have Grindr," he shouts.

I tell him that yes, I do, and ask what is wrong with that. He slurs a brief tirade about gays in big cities and promiscuity and then wants to find out specific details, such as how many Favorite profiles I have currently saved on my Grindr and whether I send naked pictures of myself out. I tell him that I don't know how many Favorites I have and that, yes, I have sent naked pictures out before. At this point he gets so repulsed by me that he leaves the living room where we're eating and shuts himself in the bedroom.

After a while he comes out and says that we should just stop talking about this and move on. I say the same thing. This lasts about two minutes and then he asks specifically what pictures I've sent. I tell him that I don't understand what the problem is and what it has to do with him, anyway. I add that he himself has sent me naked pictures and videos in the last month while we were talking, and he hadn't even met me yet. He says that I'm different, because he really liked me and then goes on to inform me that he's never ever downloaded Grindr on his phone and he hates all that social media bullshit anyway, he doesn't even do Facebook. I say that I find that hard to believe, seeing as he has thousands of friends on there, plus that's how he initially contacted me, and once again he walks away from me, this time to grab a pillow from the bedroom, come back, turn the light off, fall on the couch, and shout that I can go to sleep in the bedroom alone before he passes out.

A few hours later in the middle of the night he walks sheepishly into the bedroom where I'm lying awake, apologizes for losing his temper, kisses me on the lips, and falls asleep next to me. We wake up, hang out at home for a bit being all sweet, as if nothing happened the night before, and then he drives me to the airport to catch my return flight to California.

21

Willa and Paul have gone away on some weekend trip some-where and on Saturday afternoon my friend Chris comes over to hang out. I met Chris at the gym a few weeks ago. He's also relatively new to San Francisco, having moved here from Bos-ton, and he doesn't know many people, plus we're luckily not attracted to each other, so we just fooled around once and now we can be friends. We watch some terrible movie that he wants us to watch and do beauty treatments that we find in Willa's bathroom, and normally guys post Instagram pictures if they happen to be wearing some weird green mud face mask, because it's such an "interesting" juxtaposition of their mascu-linity with being in touch with their feminine side, but on this occasion I'd rather Willa didn't know we've been raiding her cabinets and using her stuff, so we don't post anything.

Later we go shopping for some clothes and some records and neither of us buys any clothes or records, but the shopping trip is not wasted because we do see an insanely hot guy and follow him around for a while, feeling inadequate. The things to know about this guy when we first see him from behind is that he has a big round ass, ridiculous calves, like he's spent his entire life bicycle sprint racing (and I'm going to assume that he has, for extra thrills), and is wearing knee-length shorts, boat shoes with white ankle socks that are peeking out, and a large, thick sweatshirt that fits terribly and must be way too warm for this kind of weather (summer has finally arrived in San Francisco). This upsets me very much, because he's that hot despite disguising half his body underneath baggy, unflattering clothes and wearing white sports socks that don't make any sense, i.e., he's coming across as if he doesn't care how he looks at all. Chris points out that these straight guys' "I don't care what I'm wearing" looks are probably as contrived as the average gay guy's meticulously put-together masc musc look, and this makes me feel a little better, but only until the guy turns around and I see that his face matches the color of his sandy blond hair: everything is practically monochrome, hair, tan, lips, with the only flash of color coming from his soft, blue eyes. The guy is an Olympic sprint cyclist with a permanently applied Nashville Instagram filter, and I am depressed again.

"Do you think we're a little pathetic crushing on hot, straight guys who are ten years younger than us?"

"We are very pathetic. But what can you do?"

"My biggest fear is that I'll end up like those older men who prey on young dudes and try to connect with them on a bro level. And it's embarrassing for everyone involved."

"I know what you mean. Just like that old guy in the gym who goes up to every single hot twenty-five-year-old, trying to act all young, but in fact he's doing all the young things that were cool in his time, like wearing tight Abercrombie T-shirts and having tribal bicep tattoos."

"I am that guy already. Apart from I don't talk to anyone, I just stare at them from a distance."

"By the time you're fifty-five you'll have nothing to lose though. So you will go and talk to them."

"It's terrifying how inevitable that is."

Then as we're still walking around I get a text message from Lloyd, asking what I'm up to. I tell him that I'm hanging with my friend Chris.

Lloyd: I can't stop thinking about you.
Me: I keep thinking about you too.
Lloyd: I'm glad to hear that. My feelings are very strong tho.
Lloyd: I think that I love you.
Me: Wait a minute. I believe that "being in love" with somebody is different from "loving" somebody. "Loving" somebody comes with time. So which one do you mean?
Lloyd: I'm both in love with you and I love you.

I read this whole exchange out loud to Chris.

"Is this the guy you just visited in Buffalo last week?" Chris asks.

"Yes."

"Konrad. You in danger, girl."

22

On Monday there isn't that much happening, because it's like every other day, and for that reason I am sitting here in Willa and Paul's living room and chatting to Anthony back in LA. This is a real emergency, apparently, and for that reason he tried to FaceTime me a couple times but I didn't want to do that, so we made a compromise to text instead. Anthony's emergency is from his Sunday Funday outing in WeHo's gay bars yesterday, and I know already of course that this isn't an emergency at all, but I'm here and I'm willing to listen, because what else do I have to do?

Anthony's situation right now is this: he has stopped working as a go-go dancer. He is still living with and living off Markus. Markus and he have broken up and are just friends currently.

Anthony has been in LA for only a few months and he's young and attractive and he's still stuck at that stage where he thinks that all these silly gay adventures that he finds himself engaging in have never happened to anyone in the history of the universe before and will never happen again, and honestly his life is so complicated right now that he ought to write a book about it, or so he says. Also he's tired of all this drama and the sleeping around and he wants to find a serious boyfriend and go out much less, if at all, but everyone is really shallow and not relationship-orientated and they just want to have sex with him and then move on to the next person and why can't he find someone who is as mature and over it as he is and wants the same thing?

So Anthony starts telling me his story from Sunday, and the best way that he feels he can possibly deliver the whirlwind of events and emotion that is his life right now is through a list. And he types:

1. I'm sick
2. Ran into five past hookups
3. Markus was also out and he was a shitshow
4. Left to go hook up with Eric and I couldn't get off so I left
5. Then I went back to Here bar

I write back:

1. You should probably drink less
2. You and everyone else who went out, I'm sure
3. I'm going to stop commenting completely if you keep making such obvious statements
4. [Expressionless emoji]
5. Mess

I don't like using the word "mess" but I understand from the boys of the Popjustice message board that it's multipurpose and can be inserted anywhere to convey disapproval with a camp, raised eyebrow and I think that someone like Anthony would appreciate this right now.

Then Anthony hasn't finished with his list of high emergency events that happened yesterday, so he continues:

6. Victor cornered me and wanted to know why he wasn't good enough for me
7. This random kept trying to make out with me and then found me on FB this morning
8. I talked to Aaron and he wants to get together this week [emoji of sassy brunette girl with arms crossed in front of her body to convey refusal]

Then I reply:

6. Who is Victor? (I just woke up, sorry if this is obvious)
7. This sentence can be said by 840 people in WeHo this morning
8. This sentence can be said by 840 people in WeHo this morning

Then Anthony writes: "You are so witty in the morning," because I didn't take his stories seriously enough and then I write: "I'm sorry, I just don't see any emergencies there. This is a very predictable phase of having a crazy old time going out/socializing/hooking up, which is punctuated by feelings of remorse, then repeated ad infinitum. It will be your life for the next ten years [heart kiss emoji]."

Then Anthony doesn't say anything back and then I start messaging Lloyd instead, who continues to say all the right things to me and is completely ready for serious commitment and over the gay scene and I'm so lucky that he came into my life to save me and none of this will ever end up in a complete disaster, not at all.

During the text messaging Lloyd suggests that we play a game and this is a game he calls "hypotheticals." For hypotheticals, one of us has to come up with an imaginary scenario that might occur when we're boyfriends and living in the same city and the other person has to respond with how he would react if this scenario came to be. This, apparently, is a way for us to find out more about each other. It's also a trap that Lloyd is setting up so he can get mad at me when my answer doesn't fit within the moral, antigay-scene, heteronormative ideals he so dearly holds close to his heart.

First off, he's concerned that I'm too obsessed with going to the gym and thinks that this might be detrimental to my social life and personal relationships, so he presents me with the following hypothetical:

"We are both living in California. It's Wednesday evening and one of my close friends from Buffalo is in town for one night only and wants to meet up with us and go have dinner, spend some time together. You have worked all day and usually go to the gym in the evening, but what do you do now? Do you still go to the gym and miss hanging out with us, or do you skip the gym for one day?"

I pause and think for a second.

"I would probably go to the gym quickly and then meet up with you and your friend and do whatever you want to do."

"Hm not sure I like that. Sounds like all the other big city gays who only care about their looks."

"You go to the gym as much as I do?"

"Sorry Konrad I'm not like that. For me family and friends always come first ALWSYS."

Then I panic a bit and say:

"You're right. I shouldn't care about going to the gym every day. I don't want to be that person. Can I retract my answer please? I would totally skip and hang out with you and your friend [sideways smirk emoji]."

A few hypotheticals later, I start discussing living in San Francisco.

"I've been thinking recently that San Francisco is probably not where I want to stay in the long-term."

"Whys that?"

"It's just a whole different set of people. Plus I don't really like the weather at all and if I'm going to have to walk around wearing long sleeves in the summer all the time, I might as well move back to London, which I love."

"I get that, so where will you move tho?"

"I'm starting to think about going back to LA. Trying that out again."

"I told you I'm not a big fan of LA. Everyone out there is so Hollywood. They're not good people."

"But if you were there with a boyfriend it would be a completely different experience. We won't have to do any of the scene stuff."

"Maybe your right. At the end of the day I would move anywhere to be with you."

"You're very sweet. I think we would be happy there."

"I know we would," he says. "Who do you think are the five hottest gay guys in LA?"

I have no idea how to answer that or why he's asking me, and we eventually say good night and hang up.

THIS IS IT

There will be a key moment in your life when you're thirty-three and have started to lose your looks and some of your wit and you haven't been as successful or rich as you once thought you might be and you haven't even been around your family that much since you were sixteen and you've made several wrong decisions that have left you living alone on a new continent surrounded by people who either don't know you that well and don't care about you or know you pretty well but care even less and you'll be fully aware that the nearest people who truly love you are 5,400 miles away. When you will consider that this is it, things couldn't possibly get worse, you've seriously reached the bottom and the only possible way is up. Then you'll get to the gym on a Tuesday afternoon for an intense leg workout and the left earbud in your cheap Sony headphones will have inexplicably stopped working. And this is something that you're going to have to deal with.

23

On Thursday evening I get on my bike and I go to the gym and the best thing that happens at the gym is that right at the end, when I'm doing my sit-ups, some genuine bro with pale, white skin, a very nice straight nose, and spectacular biceps comes and sits next to me and starts doing crunches, then gets his phone out and orders a pizza for delivery.

I have no idea where these bros are going to stop, where they're willing to push the limits to, but they can rest assured that I will always fall for it. I also don't even know how they come up with these inventions. Ordering a half Hawaiian, half Meat Lovers pizza with extra cheese in the gym, mid-abdominal crunch. They are killing me.

Then I go home.

In the middle of the night I wake up with a bad dream about Brett and his new boyfriend, which has become a new nightly routine, and stay up for a couple of hours, during which I make a sandwich, obsess, watch a couple episodes of *Frasier* and freak out some, before passing out again around 7:00 A.M.

The next day I meet up with Chris, still my only gay friend in San Francisco, and we go bowling, because this is something that counts as a sport, barely, and I will try every sport until I find one that I am not terrible at, so that I can possibly reassure myself a little bit about my own masculinity.

During this bowling outing we talk about vacations, celebrity CrossFit athletes, and the futileness of existence despite great wealth, because what else would two white, North American, adult gay men with no real problems talk about, and then we get to relationships.

I update Chris on Lloyd and tell him that we are now officially boyfriends and that I'm really putting the pressure on him to move to LA with me as soon as possible, because I've definitely made up my mind that I want to go back there. I also tell Chris that sometimes I have second thoughts about Lloyd, because he cannot seriously be as pure and perfect as he makes himself out to be, plus I've caught him out on a couple of lies already that concerned major things like his job and his previous relationships, etc., but he weighs over 220 pounds and it's all muscle, plus he wears button-down shirts, visors, and boat shoes, and has light eyes and is therefore a god, not to mention that he's insolent as fuck and often goes whole days ignoring my calls, but then comes back and likes all my Instagram pictures, which means that he's a sociopath who loves games and is consequently made for me.

Then the bowling comes to an end and I'm not very good, though I might just need to keep practicing, and we leave.

24

On Sunday Chris and I drive down to Los Altos Hills where a big gay pool party is being held at some rich guy's property there, primarily because we're bored of just hanging out with each other. The party started on Saturday afternoon, and lots of people arrived, several people left, a few stayed overnight, but now it's getting a second wind on this bright Sunday morning. None of the people here look like they've had anything to sustain them all weekend apart from water and pills.

Every single gay person that I've worked out next to in the gym and everyone I have gone on disastrous dates with since I moved to San Francisco is attending. There are nearly a hundred people in the house, hiding in rooms, splayed on couches, sharing showers, throwing each other in the pool, trying on sunglasses, Snapchatting, smoking pot, swapping swimwear, crushing pills, embracing in beds, taking pictures, dancing, shuffling, fucking, snorting.

I'm walking around with Chris looking for the next free hit

from someone or the next person we want to talk to. As it happens, the two are never combined. At some point, I come across the tall guy that I met in the club once who looks like Brandon from Sean Cody. He's here with his friends in the threeway relationship again. I can't do anything with him, because I am now in this imaginary long-distance relationship with Lloyd, but it doesn't hurt to hang out with someone attractive.

Brandon is really out of it. I walk up to him and say hi and he seems to recognize me, but he doesn't remember my name, so I introduce myself again. He repeats my name three times without giving me his. This is his state of mind.

"Are you in a k-hole?" I ask him.

"Ketamine," he says and his face lights up.

A few minutes into our one-sided conversation, which involves me attempting some innocuous statements about how fun this party is and him smiling at me moronically with eyes that can't focus, I grab my phone, pull the back of his board shorts out, and take a picture of his ass from above. He laughs and pushes me away with a hand that's actually gripping my shirt, not letting go, so I do it again. This time, he asks to take a look at the pictures and deletes the worst one. This is quite impressive, as it at least indicates that he's able to connect with his surroundings enough to do something.

I spot Chris sitting in the hot tub with the steroid guy I couldn't get it up for who doesn't know the difference between German and Latin. I raise my arm to get Chris's attention, and when he looks over I point down at Brandon and signal that we're coming over. The steroid guy is really friendly this time, as we're all very high and have reverted back to being best friends.

"How long have you been here?" I ask him.

"Oh I got here yesterday afternoon, bro. Been a loooooong weekend."

"Nice."

Then just as I'm about to climb into the hot tub my phone rings. It's Lloyd. I leave Brandon there with Chris and Steroid Guy and walk away to answer it.

"Hello, my love."

"What's up. I miss you. How's your Sunday?"

"It's been pretty cool. I'm hungry though. I don't think they have any food here."

"Where are you?"

"I'm at this pool party in Los Altos Hills."

There's a long, dissatisfied pause. "Aight, I'm gonna go then."

"OK, I'll talk to you later."

I go use one of the bathrooms and take some more coke and then find the others. Chris and Steroid Guy are wearing Indian headdresses that they must have found somewhere. They also now have these big, fuck-off water pistols. I see a spare one on the floor and pick it up. Chris and Steroid Guy have chased Brandon into the living room and are aggressively squirting water all over him. He's trapped in a corner between two full-length wall mirrors. All four of them, including another guy I've never seen before who's taking a movie of this on his phone, are laughing hysterically. I shoot a large stream of water straight at the new guy's face, causing him to lose his grip and drop the phone on the marble floor. The screen cracks on impact but remains in place. He picks up the phone and points it back at Brandon in the corner, who's now down on his knees.

25

In the early hours of Wednesday morning I'm lying in bed watching the finale of *The Great British Bake Off* and then when that's over and I still can't sleep I put on the 1963 film *Contempt* and halfway through that my sleeping pills finally kick in and I pass out. I wake up in the late morning and finish watching the film, then do some work and go to the gym. In the evening I go out and pick up three pizzas with Willa and Paul and then come home and eat them, though I did forget to buy Coke and I really like drinking Coke with my pizza.

I'm "bulking," but I don't feel I can pull off that term for myself, as it depends on results and I don't feel confident enough that I will achieve them. It takes a good couple of hours to get through this and I continue eating way past the point where I'm completely full, but I'm trying to enhance my importance and impact on this planet by increasing my physical mass, seeing that this seems to be the only thing anyone cares about.

On Thursday I go and have lunch at my third favorite restaurant in San Francisco and then I go to the gym.

The most important thing that happens in the gym is that
when I go to the locker room after to get changed and leave,
two bros are there talking and those two bros are: (1) the pizza
bro from last week who was doing sit-ups and simultaneously
ordering a pizza for delivery on the phone, (2) another bro I
see every evening who has a blond beard, nice muscles, and
exclusively listens to some stupid hard-core metal shit that
makes him head-bang consistently throughout all his workouts. The conversation between those two bros, who seem like
they haven't spoken before, goes like this:

> Pizza bro: "You look so big, bro."
> Hard-core bro: "Thanks, man, I been bulking, so."
> Hard-core bro after a brief pause: "Do I really look bigger?"
> Pizza bro: "Yeah, you look huge."
> Hard-core bro: "Thanks, man. And I haven't even been
>   training as much as I want."
> Pizza bro: "How many days do you lift?"

Then I leave before they start making out and punch myself
in the face for not being man enough to ever speak to either of
them, though perhaps they don't want to speak to me, because
they can tell I'm gay and they prefer their homosexual banter
safe, heterosexual, and leading nowhere.

When I come out of the gym I text Chris and tell him ex-

actly what just occurred in the gym and finish my message
with: "EVERYOBE IS BULKIN. EVERYONE IS A BRO.
EVERRYONE IS PERFECT. I WANT THEM ALL."

Chris: Can we just get them all together (possibly drug
        them if we have to) and have an orgy. And why do
        you disappoint me by not getting a pic of these beau-
        tiful men?
Me: I thought about it but their beauty was paralyzing.
Chris: If you see them again, you must.
Me: I'll try. I'm so glad we're ahead of the curve with our
        bulking though. I feel like for once, we've tapped
        into a real trend early on and we're making good
        progress.

On Friday night I go to the cinema with Chris to watch
This Is Where I Leave You and I dare him to ask for two tickets
to *Dis Where I Leave You* but he doesn't and this really disap-
points me, because I know that Hard-core Bro would.

After the film I go back home and talk to Lloyd on the
phone and announce to him that I'm moving back to LA in
less than a month, but I will be living on the beach this time,
and insist that he also move there before the end of the year to
be with me, otherwise we're going to have to break up.

26

On Saturday I move into my new place in Venice. It's a one-bedroom flat at the top of a small, two-floor complex, three blocks from the beach. There is a courtyard in the middle with a small swimming pool, the building manager lives on the ground floor with his girlfriend, who has pink hair and thinks she's a punk, and a lot of the residents keep surfboards on their balconies. I think I like it.

The first thing I did was get Wi-Fi installed. I had the technician come in yesterday, before I even moved in. I would rather have had Wi-Fi than running water. Today my mattress also arrived, and I just put it on the bedroom floor. I don't have a frame yet. The mattress is a queen size. I might have gotten a king size, because of my ridiculous sleeping problems and always wanting to move around, but Lloyd complained that with a king mattress we would be spending the night too far from each other and we wouldn't be able to cuddle. So I didn't.

I have zero other furniture. I'm waiting for Lloyd to arrive,

so we can go and buy everything together. He has agreed to
quit his job and leave everything behind and move to LA for
me next month.

My kitchen window is facing inside the building, and
across the courtyard I can see the kitchen window and front
door of the flat directly opposite mine. This evening, they are
keeping the front door open. There is quiet music coming out
of their living room. I understand that a young couple in their
late twenties lives there, and tonight they are having a party. I
stand in my kitchen with the lights off and look across for a
while. It would seem that it's the boyfriend's birthday. He is
short, with dark hair and glasses and he's dressed too warmly
for the weather. The girlfriend is the exact opposite. She is
blond and surfery and looks like she just came straight from
the beach. In the half hour that I stand and watch in the dark,
a few of my other neighbors walk over to the flat, some carry-
ing gifts or bottles, and join the party. Most people that I see
are up to thirty-five or so, and almost all of them are couples.
Possibly one day soon these people will be my friends.

I have nothing to do this evening, so I take my bike and
ride the three blocks over to the beach. The Venice boardwalk
is busy as ever, but as I ride north on the bike path, up toward
Santa Monica and past the pier, it gets a lot quieter and a lot
darker. Soon the only light around me comes from the head-
light on my bike, and the only people I come across are evening joggers or small groups of skateboarder kids practicing
and getting stoned on the beach.

I'm listening to a playlist with old songs that made me sad
back when I was very young, when I was still living in Berlin,

by bands like the Smiths, Suede, and Gene, hoping for a similar feeling now at thirty-three. This works pretty well, with added layers of sadness because I now know a lot more about the passing of time and empty lives, and I soon reach a very satisfactory level of nearly tearful nostalgia. This is probably my most content emotional state, especially when it's caused by circumstances I've deliberately created to trigger it, like I'm doing now, as opposed to uncontrollable situations that happen around me and I fall victim to.

My ride lasts an hour or so. I think about Brett a lot, think about his new life and wonder if he's happy and whether he actually ever thinks of me, if he misses me sometimes.

On the way back, on the same bike path as I get closer to Venice again, I ride by ten-million-dollar homes right on the oceanfront, so I slow down to look inside. People's lights are on, they're home for the evening, and I see some of them in their kitchens, in their living rooms, couples and families and friends with their perfect lives in their perfect homes. I text Chris and complain about them a little bit, and ask why our lives aren't perfect like that. Chris writes back and he says, "Do you not think that maybe some people look at you and think you have a perfect life? People who see your Instagram?" And I say, "Yeah, maybe they do." And Chris says, "Right, and look at how shitty your life is, you idiot," and I take the point and I go back home.

From there, I give Lloyd a call. It's 1:00 A.M. on the East Coast. I know that he's gone out. He doesn't answer his phone the two times that I call and finally calls me back an hour later. He's driving back home, he says. He didn't answer before because he'd forgotten his phone in a friend's car. He's very,

very drunk and decides to launch into a story about the U.S. government and all the secrets that they're keeping from us, something about aliens, something about terrorism, and then a lot more stuff about aliens, then we eventually hang up when he arrives home.

27

On Saturday afternoon, Peter Henderson comes over to the beach and picks me up to go on a hike at a place called Point Dume in Malibu. Peter is one of Anthony's friends that I met here in LA before I went away. Unlike Anthony and his go-go dancing, Peter seems to have a job where he has to use his brain, barely, producing reality TV. He moved here for school from a small town in Ohio over a decade ago, and I guess once you move away from a small town in Ohio, you never go back. I'm going to try to be his friend so that I don't spend every single minute in Southern California alone until Lloyd arrives to save me. The hike goes well. Peter seems nice enough and as a bonus I am not sexually attracted to him, which is very promising for our potential friendship. When Peter gets tired of hanging out with a depressive misanthrope on the west side, he goes back to Hollywood where he lives and I go back to my flat in Venice.

I talk to Lloyd and tell him that I went on a hike with a new friend and Lloyd tells me that it sounds like I went on a date actually and gets mad at me and then I reassure him that it absolutely wasn't a date and what am I supposed to do, lock myself in the house and not talk to anyone? That's what I do most of the time anyway. Then Lloyd calms down a little bit even though he's still not happy, he says, and asks me how I'm finding LA anyway now that I'm back there and I say that I guess it's OK but it will be a lot better when he's there with me next month and then Lloyd says he can't wait either but he'd rather I didn't live in such a gay area as Venice. I tell him that Venice is not a gay area specifically and what is he talking about, and he says that he's heard that Venice is gay enough and if it were up to him he would be living somewhere like Manhattan Beach, and I say, well OK, I guess I'm gayer than he is and he's a genuine masc nonscene bro and he can move to Manhattan Beach if he likes when he gets here. Then he says that he might, asks me again who the top five sexiest guys in LA are, if I were to make a list. I fail to come up with any names because (a) I don't care, (b) I'm blindly in lust with him and no one else seems attractive, and we hang up.

In the evening of my second Saturday back in LA I sit at home and take a few bumps of ketamine and listen to the album *Halfaxa* by Grimes all the way through and then I get in my car and go grocery shopping in a supermarket that's not the nearest to my house, but the second nearest, because I wanted to drive. When I come out of the store with all my bags I put them in the trunk and then I sit in my car for a bit in the parking lot and it's after 10:00 P.M. and I cry for a bit, because this is all I ever wanted to have, someone to go grocery shopping with me on a Saturday night and I guess here I am and I don't, then I get over this and drive home.

28

My next-door neighbor, Elvira, is a middle-aged lady who has modeled her life on the mannerisms and general demeanor of Diane Keaton, only with even more of that contrived, stammering ditziness, if that's humanly possible, and with the added toll taken by several decades of living in a small, rent-controlled beach apartment while watching life pass you by. She came over and introduced herself two weeks after I moved in by asking, "Do you have a cold because I can hear you sneeze through the wall?" So she keeps pretty close track of what goes on in my apartment. Sneezing, my phone ringing, clipping nails: she keeps a tab on everything.

So after she came over and introduced herself, the floodgates of intrusiveness opened. What was previously quiet espionage was now explicit surveillance. I certainly don't think I'm special to her in those terms, I'm pretty sure she keeps an eye on everyone in the building, it's just that I make it particularly easy for her by living right next door. If I play along to this close relationship that she wants us to have, it's all fine.

Please note, based on her suggestions over the time we've known each other, the close relationship that she wants us to have includes keeping our front doors open so the other person can come in and out and chat at their will, getting high together on evenings when we're bored, and giving the other person a key to our apartment, "for emergencies," every time we go away for the weekend. When I don't play along and try to maintain some privacy or establish some barriers, I see the other, nonhippy side of her.

One of her most unfortunate habits (unfortunate for me) is that she loves to stand outside my kitchen window and talk to me while I prepare food, wash dishes, or whatever. I find this to be almost a criminal violation. One time, she was walking past my window as I was walking away and we caught a glimpse of each other. Because it all happened too quickly and we didn't have the chance to talk to each other, she stopped walking, put her hands on either side of her face to shield away any reflections on the glass, and stuck her nose to the outside of my window, so she could follow me around and see where I was going inside my apartment. This was a bit too much, and even as insipid and socially inept as I am, I decided to complain to her. Then, I kept the kitchen window curtains closed for a few days, just to drive the point home. During those days, each time she saw me coming in or out of my apartment she refused to acknowledge me at all. At the end of the week, as I was leaving, she heard me, burst out of her apartment, and told me that everyone in the building hates me because I bang my front door every time I come in or out, and would I mind being a bit more quiet, thank you very much. The next day I opened my curtains again, because I didn't want the grief. Our friendship was reinstated immediately after that.

The problem with all this, sadly, is that my neighbor is just the female version of me in twenty-five years. During our frequent one-sided catch-ups, she has often shared stories of her youth, referring to herself as a former "beach babe," mentioning surfing adventures, carefree trips along the California coast, and flings with men who ended up being wrong for her. Please tell me that this isn't me. Please give me a guarantee that I won't be here, living in this same apartment at fifty-eight, unemployed, aimless, and insane, occupying myself with peeking through my neighbors' windows, trying to live vicariously through them. So sometimes, for extremely selfish reasons and in the hope that in the future when I am Elvira my young neighbors will do the same for me, I think that I should probably humor her, be friendly, and give her some attention. Other times, and despite my occasional good intentions, she makes this very difficult.

On this Wednesday evening, I'm home alone and trying to pull myself away from refreshing Facebook and go to bed. It's minutes before midnight.

I hear a knock on the door, and of course I know it's Elvira and I seriously consider not answering, but she knocks again, more fervently this time, and I know this is just not going to go away.

I open the door and she storms in holding a candlestick like a weapon. She's sorry she had to bother me, she says, unclear whether she's more or less sorry compared to the other five times she did it in the last couple of weeks, with an urgent story of low-stake apartment building warfare somehow connected to her self-assigned role as neighborhood watch official, but something really disturbing is happening and she needs my help.

I almost say "what is it," but in reality this is not a discussion where my input is needed, she can continue the dialogue for both of us, just taking minor cues from my facial expressions or stance: half a raised eyebrow here, a minor shift of my eyeballs there, blinking, shifting the weight between my legs as I stand there otherwise inanimate, it all counts as my part of the conversation.

This time she tells me that she's heard some noises and wants me to go investigate the apartment downstairs from hers, because she thinks someone is getting murdered very quietly, or having violent sex very quietly, both of which she thinks she can help with. I say no. She says, fine, if she goes downstairs and someone is getting murdered and she gets caught up herself I will have it on my conscience, and my silence must indicate that I'm fine with that, because she leaves, candlestick in hand, and heads down the corridor.

I listen out for approximately two seconds and I hear nothing, so I go to bed.

29

Early Friday evening, after almost a week's drive across the country, Lloyd finally arrives in LA. I can now start leading a very happy existence, seeing that he is my only source of happiness. I go downstairs to greet him and let him in. He's even more attractive in real life than I remember. I help him carry his stuff upstairs from his car and then offer him his favorite beer, a huge supply of which I bought to welcome him. He tells me that he doesn't want to drink it right now; in fact he's considering that he will stop drinking alcohol for at least a year, now that he's moved here, because he really wants to turn his life around, become successful, stop falling victim to all the distractions and young behavior that he's been trapped in, not to mention that it's gay people who go to all the bars and clubs and are part of the scene that get wasted all the time and take drugs, and he doesn't want to be one of them. I say, oh OK then, and put the beer back in the fridge. We kiss each other for a little bit, but then he says he's really tired and wants to sleep very early, which makes sense, so he showers and goes to bed. I walk down to Abbot Kinney and have dinner by myself and also bring some home for him in case he wakes up and gets hungry.

On Saturday after we wake up I make breakfast and he starts unpacking and putting his things away. I've left half of all closet and storage spaces empty for him. When most of that is done (he hasn't brought many things at all) I attempt to make out with him and possibly fuck, but he tells me that he hasn't been to the gym in a week because he was driving across the whole country to get here and his body looks like shit at the moment, so I'm not allowed to see him naked, nor am I allowed to touch him, so we'll have to wait. I reassure him that his body looks fine to me and question what possible difference five days of not working out could possibly have made, but he is adamant and I give up. Once he gets back into his gym routine and rebuilds his body, he says, we can get naked.

Peter then comes over to meet us for lunch. We drive over to Main Street in Santa Monica and sit at a place called The Gallery. I am immensely happy that I now have a boyfriend and a friend who want to do boring stuff like that with me. Why was I so upset over Brett leaving me? Clearly we wanted different things and were never meant to be together. Halfway through the lunch, Lloyd says that he's gonna go over to LA and meet up with some friends. I ask who these friends might be and he says, Daniel, Rus, and X, which makes sense, as they are the only people he knows in the city. Somehow I don't particularly like the fact that this is happening and I'd love to go with him and check the situation out, but I don't really want to be a highly paranoid, suspicious, and controlling boyfriend (even though I am), so I let him go and I stay on the west side with Peter. A couple of hours later, Peter also leaves.

Around 8:00 P.M., and having not heard anything from Lloyd all day, I text him to see what he's up to. At this point I'm so bored and alone that I want to go meet him and even go out with him in West Hollywood if that's what he wants. He texts back half an hour later with the following message:

"Heyy bub im with myfreinds how;s yo"

Even for someone expectedly inarticulate that seems a bit much, so I text back with a simple "What?" He doesn't respond and then about an hour later, I give him a call. He answers from a place where really loud music is playing and I can hardly hear him. I make something out about Daniel, Rus, X, and I ask where he is and if I can come join them. I can't hear any more of his answers and then the call drops. "The call drops" is code that I use on myself to make the fact that he hung up on me sound better. I text him immediately, quite furious, and ask what the hell he's thinking leaving me by myself all day on his first weekend in LA and going to hang out instead with the people he's been having orgies with in the past. He texts back with:

"rOrgies? Goodbye Konrd"

I spend the next hour calling his mobile and texting him but I don't get any response and then eventually decide to leave the house and go to the gym. My blood is boiling. In the parking garage at the gym I'm so distracted and mad that I drive my car into a pillar while taking a left turn and create a big dent on my door, and then I work out.

Lloyd comes back home at eleven thirty the next morning. He looks like death. Who am I kidding, he still looks like some sort of god and I would kill every living relative I have outside my mum to (a) have sex with him, and (b) be seen out in a public place with him. He says that he's sorry and that he got upset with me because I was making accusations while he was just out, spending time with his friends. For some reason he got really drunk, he says, and he thinks that somebody probably spiked his drink with drugs, because it doesn't make any sense otherwise. He really didn't drink all that much. I say that that's bullshit, he started drinking at midday and it makes perfect sense how he would have gotten so drunk by the evening, add that this is a perfect start to his plan to turn his life around and become more responsible in LA, and ask if he thinks his parents would be proud of him. This seems to touch a nerve and he jumps up from my bed where he's been hiding under a blanket because he's hungover as hell and mostly unable to move and he tells me that that's it, we're done and he's moving out, and makes a halfhearted attempt to grab a bag and throw his stuff in. I start crying and begging him to forgive me, I didn't mean what I said, so he forgives me and goes back to bed.

I suddenly recall that he once told me during our extensive long-distance interaction that he gets particularly horny the next day after a big night out after his hangover has subsided a bit, so I leave him to sleep for a couple of hours, then get naked and get into bed with him. I start pulling his clothes off and trying to kiss him. At this point I realize that he's not wearing any underwear, even though he's still wearing the clothes he was wearing when he left yesterday. There are two possibilities here: either he left his underwear somewhere in the last thirty-six hours that he's been out, or he left to go to the gay bars without wearing any underwear to start with, and I don't know which scenario is giving me the biggest aneurism, but either way I choose to ignore the fact for now and continue my attempt at acquiring a sex life. He regains full consciousness for a moment while I'm sucking his dick, which is surprisingly hard, just to push me away. I leave him to sleep and go jerk off in the bathroom, thinking of his perfect, unconscious body lying on my bed and then spend the rest of the day taking turns between reading a book in the next room and going to look at him to regain inspiration and jerk off again while I wait for him to wake up. By 6:00 P.M. when he emerges from the bedroom, I have cum four times.

30

On Monday I have about half a day's work to do. Lloyd wakes up and sits on the opposite side of the living room, looking for jobs on his laptop. He has been here for over two weeks now and even though he has joined a gym again and started working out, our sex life remains elusive. He has also taken to building a barrier comprising two pillows between us when we sleep, which is a far cry from the days when he was asking me all the way from Buffalo not to buy a king-size mattress because we wouldn't be able to cuddle, but I fear that at this stage there isn't even a remote correlation between what was being said then and what is happening now.

The gym he has joined is different from the one I go to, it's all the way over in Hollywood and he has to drive forty minutes to get there with no traffic.

"I wanna lift somewhere else 'cause I want to go there, get in the zone, and do my own thing," he said. "Just because we're boyfriends doesn't mean we have to be joined at the hip."

"That makes sense," I said.

"In fact, relationships are stronger when two people have their own lives and just get together to enjoy each other's company whenever they want to. That's the sign of a good relationship," he told me soon after he got here.

Well, we now don't work out together, we don't go out together, and we don't have almost any physical contact, so our relationship must be pretty fucking solid.

On this Monday, his job hunt remains on a very perfunctory level, which at least shows a sign of consistency that I've really come to admire about his character in the time that he's spent here, and he soon switches to his favorite daytime activity: making a music playlist to accompany his afternoon workout. This is an activity that takes up three or four hours every day. It seems to be extremely important for the music that he listens to in the gym to change every day and it's meticulously selected and put together, so much so that I really find it hard to imagine how he could also fit an actual job in his day. Perhaps that is why he is avoiding getting one.

When that's done and I'm finally spared continuous bursts of brief segments of songs he's trying out coming from the tinny speakers of his shitty old laptop, he continues to sit there, this time playing with his phone. The phone starts buzzing at an alarming rate, indicating an influx of text messages that I, personally, have only experienced when I'm trapped in a group iMessage with seventy-five other people. When I ask him who's sending all these messages, because I'm a very open-minded, noncontrolling boyfriend if I'm anything, he responds that he's decided to text everyone who appears in his contacts as a first-name entry only and if he can't remember where he met them, to enquire about their connection. Yes, that is my brand-new boyfriend who refuses to have sex with me, hitting up all his previous hookups. Before all my blood rises to my head I decide to take a break and go outside to pick up some lunch.

When I come back with food for both of us, I find him blasting his gym playlist from the living room stereo and dancing around. We sit down at the dining table to eat, but as soon as we've started "Gas Pedal" by Sage the Gemini comes on and this causes him to exclaim "wooooooooh" very loudly, put his fork down, raise his arms up in the air, and start grinding heavily on the chair. The combination of his exposed blond hairy armpits, his biceps, which he's flexing above his head, and the fact that he's grinding so hard that it's a genuine miracle the chair doesn't disappear inside his enormous, muscular ass leaves me so intensely horny that it becomes almost impossible to breathe. Any doubts that I ever had about this relationship are put to the side. I will do anything for this guy as long as I live. He can stay here at my place forever. He can continue being repulsed by me and avoid touching me, but I will continue feeding him and sheltering him as long as I'm given the privilege of being allowed to look at him this close up. He is a god.

Because of my horny delirium, I make another futile attempt at physical contact. I tell him that he looks really hot and ask him if he'd like to fuck. He continues to dance and tells me that I look hot too, but I'm so obsessed with sex and need to chill out a little bit.

"Relationships are not all about sex," he says.

"I agree, but relationships are a little bit about sex and we're not having any sex at all."

The song changes to "Wiggle" by Jason Derulo. He takes his tank top off, because he's a cruel bastard, stands up, walks over to my chair, and sits on my lap, where he starts grinding on my dick.

"So you want to fuck?" he says.

"Yes."

I put my arms around him and start kissing his chest. He leans back, still grinding on my crotch, and I kiss his stomach, then pull him back up to face him and start making out with him.

No more than five seconds later, he stands up, stops the music, and puts his shirt back on. I ask him what the hell he's doing. He says that he's running late for the gym and we can continue this later. He throws his gym stuff in a bag and leaves. He comes back home hours later, just before 9:00 P.M., with no explanation as to where he's been and we don't really talk to each other until we go to bed with a pillow fortress between us.

I'm still awake at 3:00 A.M. I finally get up because this sleep thing isn't happening for me, get dressed, and go outside for a walk. It's very cold though, so instead I just sit on the steps at the building entrance and listen to a short playlist I've made, alternating songs from the albums *Overgrown* by James Blake and *Cupid Deluxe* by Blood Orange.

When I go back up, I sit on the side of the bed and wake Lloyd up. I must be visibly upset. "What's wrong, bubba?" he says. I tell him that I don't know what's going on and that I'm really unhappy. I ask him to tell me whether he likes me at all anymore. I say that I know relationships are not all about sex, but he must be able to see that this is a problem. There's no intimacy between us. He sits up to indicate that he's fully present and willing to participate in this forced heart-to-heart. He nods his head slowly, lowering his eyes, in a move that's meant to convey he understands and is equally upset. I ask him to tell me what is wrong then. If there's anything I can do to help. He doesn't speak for a few seconds and then he says that he thinks he has developed some sort of fear. He says that he can't even remember when he last had sex with anyone. I remind him that he had sex when I visited him in Buffalo back in August. He says, oh yeah, he can't even remember when he last had sex with anyone apart from the time I visited him in Buffalo back in August. Because he'd been living there for so long, he says, and he was so unhappy with his life, he stopped thinking about sex completely. Plus there really wasn't anyone around to date. Apart from that one time with me, he hasn't had sex in over a year. Maybe two years even, he can't remember. Now he's built up a wall, and it's difficult to let anyone in. He says that he finds it really upsetting, if I must know. I tell him that I wasn't aware of that and that I understand. I tell him that we can take it slow and that I'm there for him. He says great, let's go back to sleep now, and I move over to my side of the bed.

31

On this Saturday afternoon, three weeks after having lived with me, Lloyd is gracious enough to allow me to go to the same gym as him and work out at the same time, albeit not together. This is good enough for me. When we finish lifting, we decide to go in the swimming pool and maybe swim for a bit, maybe use the steam room. In preparation for this, as soon as I'm done with the weights, I go into the locker room and quickly jerk off. This should provide me with some temporary peace of mind and the ability to coexist with Lloyd in his swimming shorts without being driven completely crazy with desire, because, as has been pointed out several times, he is a god.

We swim a couple laps and then both go into the steam room. Because he is heartless or a moron, but most likely the perfect combination of both, he asks me when the last time was that I used a steam room. I say that I don't actually remember, it's probably several years ago, and I don't particularly like it; if I go to a pool I usually just swim and get out. I ask him the same thing, because that's what he wanted. He says that it was a few months ago when he was visiting D.C., and he says this in a very gleeful way that makes his whole face light up. I am masochistic enough to ask what thrilling memories he may possibly have from that steam room in D.C. and he replies that something happened there. I press on, even though I know where this is going, and where this is going is not very beneficial for the arteries surrounding my heart, but I still want to know. So, Lloyd says, he was staying in a hotel there ("Who paid for it?" is my instinctive question, but I keep my mouth shut) and one evening he went downstairs to the pool. There was just one guy swimming there, in his early forties, handsome, fit, but Lloyd didn't want to swim and went straight into the steam room. Seconds later, the handsome, fit forty-year-old also walked in and sat opposite him. The man then proceeded to open his towel and sit there with what Lloyd describes as one of the biggest dicks he's ever seen.

"It was like a baby's arm, I'm telling you."

Right at this point I'm hyperventilating from jealousy, but I want to hear the rest.

"What happened then?" I ask

"He started stroking it and staring at me."

"And then what?"

"Then I'm not telling you."

"You went and sat on it, didn't you? You slut," I helpfully offer.

"You're calling me a slut? You've had sex with two hundred people."

"Yes, but I'm not a fucking hypocrite about it."

Then Lloyd tells me off for swearing again, but I stay on

topic and inform him that I'm adding this person, the sauna guy, to the list of people he's had sex with in the last year, and yes, I have been keeping count ever since he told me about his supposed intimacy issues and alleged "sex wall." We are now at three confirmed fucks (all of which I helpfully remind him of, one by one, by repeating stories he's inadvertently told me in the last couple of weeks because he can't keep track of his own lies) and now one tentative fuck that I will corroborate sooner or later.

He tells me I'm insane and leaves the steam room.

On the drive back home, and because I cannot think of anything else right now apart from how many people this man might have had sex with, how frequently, in what positions, and why he won't have sex with me, I decide to ask him about the time that Daniel, Rus, and X flew him out to LA.

"You were here for four days," I say. "How many times did you guys fuck in that time?"

He refuses to answer. I step on the brake and bring the car to a halt in the middle of the road. There is no traffic around us, but there are cars coming up behind us in the distance.

"Are you crazy?" he says.

"Yes. I'm not moving until you answer my question."

"I don't know . . . ten maybe."

I start the car again, because we did make a deal, but I'm focusing on anything but the driving.

"You had sex ten times in three and a half fucking days?" I scream at him.

"Well, there were three of them."

I want to drive into the nearest wall, but that's not guaranteed to kill me, plus I'm getting hard and I want to hear more details.

I violently spit out a number of questions:

"So they took turns on you? Did you fuck and get fucked by each of them? Who has the biggest dick? How soon after they picked you up at the airport did you first fuck? If you got there Friday afternoon and left Monday morning and had sex ten times, that means three times per day on average. When did they all happen?"

He doesn't answer any of my questions, tells me that I'm insane a few more times, adds that I'm not allowed to ask any questions about his previous sex life ever again, and then we get home. I go to the bathroom to jerk off again and he sits in the living room to watch TV.

32

For New Year's Eve there is no particular plan, as LA people tend to leave LA and go spend New Year's somewhere else. My suggestion is that we go to this big club downtown, but Lloyd dismisses it as being "a circuit party," and as we all know he doesn't do circuit parties because he's not a typical gay.

By 8:00 P.M. we have spent the entire day saying to each other "I don't care what we do, as long as we're together," and one of us means it. Another suggestion of mine, to walk down to Santa Monica Pier and see what they have going on there, is also dismissed, so around 9:00 P.M. we end up going online and buying tickets for the club night downtown. I pay the $350 for both of them, since it was my idea apparently, plus he doesn't even have money to buy food, let alone nearly two hundred bucks to throw away on a gay circuit party.

We get to the club around 11:00 P.M. and the club is really, really packed. Unable-to-move level of packed. I buy us drinks and we walk around the periphery of the dance floor trying to find some pills to buy. This is particularly important to me, because I am living in blind faith that if Lloyd is high enough he might allow me to have sex with him when we go back home.

Within the first twenty minutes of being there, it becomes apparent that I'll be spending a very big part of the evening by myself or at best talking to strangers, because Lloyd has decided to put his favorite adage into practice again, one that he exclaimed to me in the first few days after he moved to LA "to be with me," whereby "a good couple is a couple that walks into a party together, they separate, socialize and have a good time individually without being needy, then come together again at the end of the evening and leave."

So I find us some pills, buy us some more drinks, and very shortly after I find myself standing alone, trying to find somebody to talk to, even though I am still madly infatuated by the guy who is posing as my boyfriend and living in my house, but wants to have nothing to do with me in both public or intimate situations.

Right before midnight, I make a very concentrated effort to go find him, so that at least we spend the few minutes that will take us to the new year together. The club has three floors and a few thousand people in it, but I have nothing else to do and I'm very patient, so eventually I run into him. He's hanging out with a group of people he knows who live in New York, apparently, and are visiting LA for New Year's. Because I'm very obsessive and quite single-minded and, again, I have very little to do with my life, I recognize one of the New York people as someone who Lloyd has spent a lot of time over the last few months that we've known each other liking Facebook pictures of. He is one of his thousands of Facebook friends and his perfect type, and I suppose that he might have moved to New York to live with him instead if the guy had offered, but I was lucky enough to get in there first.

I'm not the most welcome person to turn up in the group right now, I can tell, and even though Lloyd does me the favor of standing next to me at midnight, he doesn't really want to interact with me and, in fact, cuts me off every time I try to say something to him, complaining that the music is too loud and he can't hear me, so we might as well not speak. A few minutes after midnight, and just with a peck on the lips, he walks away again.

I spend the next hour by myself. In an unexpected turn of events, Lloyd then shows up complaining that he's been looking everywhere for me and says that I keep disappearing. He asks me for some cash to buy some drinks. I ask whether that's the only reason why he wanted to come find me and he becomes really offended, says, "Bub, don't even say that, you know I wanna hang out with you," takes the money, and says he's going to the bathroom and will be right back.

The next time that I see him is half an hour later when I'm standing on a balcony on the second floor, overlooking the dance floor downstairs. I spot Lloyd in the middle of the crowd, standing face-to-face with the Facebook guy from New York. People around them are dancing, walking around, talking, but they're against each other, staring into each other's eyes. My heart drops. I stand there staring at them from upstairs, in the distance. I start praying that they don't kiss. They kiss. It lasts for about two minutes, then they pull away and Lloyd looks around, scanning the room. There is no way he can see me where I am. He turns to New York again and nods to him to follow him. I watch them both make their way through the crowd and leave the dance floor.

When we leave the club a couple of hours later, Lloyd is very, very high and I suspect he has taken more pills from other people, or indeed we might have taken the same amount of drugs, but they stopped working on me after a while. His high is making him extremely arrogant and he starts a conversation outside the club, where he wanted to stay longer, about how attractive he is.

"Dayum," he shouts at me. "Everyone in this club was blowing. Me. Up."

"Yes, well done. You are very desirable."

"What is *wrong* with those people? So thirsty."

"I'm sure you hated it."

"What's wrong, boy? Jealous? 'Cause I could have anyone I wanted?"

"Yeah, a bunch of homosexuals on Ecstasy were eyeing you up. You must be very proud."

"You wanna go back in there? You wanna have a little competition?"

"Oh god."

"See who's the hottest? Let's go back in there. Ask some people to choose between us. See what they say."

We don't go back in there and ask people to choose. Instead we go home.

I get straight into bed. He goes to the bathroom, leaving his phone on the floor next to the bed, which is the biggest indicator of how out of it he really is, because it's usually always attached to his hand and nobody is allowed to touch it. While he's away, the phone keeps buzzing. The phone is locked and he has chosen the setting where the text messages arrive and pop up at the top of the screen but you can't read the first line on a locked screen, you can just see the name of the person texting you. I pick it up and look at it and see the name of the New York guy show up again and again and again.

Lloyd comes back from the bathroom and I tell him he's been getting a lot of text messages. He grabs his phone and reads them. I ask him to tell me who's texting him at 4:00 A.M. and he says that his best friend in Buffalo is drunk and missing him. I ignore his lie plus the fact that I saw him make out with a random guy at the club because I'm scared he'll get mad at me if I say anything and use it as an excuse not to have sex with me and I make a really pitiful attempt to make out with him. He tells me that I can forget it, he's had a shitty night and he's not in the mood, puts a pillow between us, and turns around to sleep.

JANUARY

33

Today is my birthday. Some people take the opportunity of their birthday to reflect, and become depressed about the passing of time and not having achieved everything they wanted to achieve in their lives yet. I do this on *any* regular day, so today is not going to be that special.

The only thing that might be different today is that Lloyd might allow me to touch him sexually, or so he has been promising to me ever since he moved here and it became apparent that we were not going to have a sex life unless some major disruption happened to the space and time continuum, like: Earth being sucked into a black hole; my birthday; or him suddenly deciding to be honest for once and telling me why he refuses to have sex with his boyfriend, but will happily do it with other people without giving it a second thought.

I mean, I know the answer of course; I'm not that much of a fool. This is a guy who's not into me at all and is just using me for the time being, and in recent weeks I've become painfully aware of this, but until he decides to man up and tell me the truth I might as well keep trying so that I can at least get some return for all the money I'm spending on him.

The day starts off promisingly. Lloyd gives me my present (two pairs of Sperrys that I loaned him money last week to go buy and are in the wrong color but that's OK, because I can go change them later) and a birthday card that reads:

> I've been thinking and want to tell you I haven't been this happy in my life. You make me the happiest person. Being around you, learning you, experiencing life with you just makes me so beyond content. The ups far outway [sic] the downs and the more I get to understand this super complex person, the more I love him. Happy birthday bub.
>
> Love, Lloyd

Then things continue a bit less promisingly, because Lloyd announces that he won't be able to join my birthday dinner this evening, as his best friend from back home is in LA for one evening only on a stopover in his road trip from San Francisco to San Diego and he's promised that he would go see him. This, of course, is lifted straight from the hypothetical scenarios he was presenting to me and we were fighting about before he moved to LA. Honestly, it's as if all these stories are completely made up.

I don't ask whether that's the same best friend who was texting him drunk in the middle of the night from Buffalo just yesterday, because I fear that he might get mad at me for uncovering his lies and then break up with me. So I say OK, but can we at least have sex after. He says, "Of course we'll have sex on your birthday, bub, what are you talking about?"

I am joined at my birthday dinner by Peter and two of his friends, who must have felt sorry for me, and then I go home and patiently wait for my birthday sex to arrive. At around 10:00 P.M. I call Lloyd to get an update and he answers really, really drunk and slurs that he was just about to drive home, but he realized he's better off waiting to sober up a little first, so right now he's sitting on the pavement right next to his car, sipping some water. I'm thinking, finally, this guy has turned around and is a responsible human being, what a dick that I have been for doubting him. At 11:30 P.M. I call again and don't get an answer. At 12:30, half an hour after my thirty-fourth birthday has expired, I stop sobbing hysterically into my pillow, take some Valium, and lie in bed awake and brain-dead. After 2:00 A.M. Lloyd comes home. I decide to play it very cool, not ask any questions, and pretend I haven't noticed what time it is.

I've never seen him so drunk in my life. Well, I've only been around him for just over two months. I haven't seen him so drunk in over two months. I'm sure he's gotten a lot more drunk and a lot more frequently, but I just wasn't around. He clearly has no memory of my birthday, my birthday sex, or what year it is. He falls on the bed and launches into an extremely loud story about driving home, then witnessing a car accident, where a maniac who must have been "high on drugs" drove into a barbershop on Santa Monica Boulevard then climbed out of his car screaming with blood on his face and ran away from his vehicle, which by that point was on fire, while

Lloyd stopped driving, waited around, and gave an eyewitness account to the police when they got there. I nod along for about half an hour while this impossible story is repeated again and again and again with small variations throughout and helpfully exclaim "oh my god," "are you serious," and "no way" at appropriate points to indicate that I'm listening, very carefully not using any swear words that I know will give him an excuse to get mad at me, then when he's done with repeating the story I make a move to kiss him and he says he just saw a man nearly die, and is sex the only thing I have on my mind? Then I lose all the patience I had collected in the last two months and tell him that I want to break up with him. He says fine, and falls asleep.

34

On Friday morning, I get up and throw some clothes in a bag. My dad and his wife are away in Hawaii, so I'm going to go spend the weekend at his house in the Palisades. I wait around for Lloyd to wake up before leaving. I want to see what he has to say and whatever it is that he has to say, I want to cling onto it and forgive him and say that I didn't mean it last night and I don't want to break up with him. Then eventually Lloyd wakes up and complains of a headache and asks me if he remembers correctly that I said something about breaking up and I kinda mince my words a little bit and say that, hey, maybe I said something like that but I was really upset because it was my birthday and I'd missed him and I don't *really* want to break up with him, and what does he think?

Then Lloyd tells me that he actually thinks it's a good idea and he's at a very transitional stage in his life where he needs to focus on himself and get his act together and only when he's happy with himself and the way his life is going will he be able to devote himself to another person and be in a good relationship, not to mention that he's in a new city and this is all too much for him to take and in summary he is now breaking up with me.

I tell him that I'm going away for the weekend so we can get a little bit of distance but he can stay at my place and I don't mind, he can take his time moving out, and then he says, before I go away, do I want to go and grab something to eat together and I say, sure, I'd love to do that and somewhere inside I think, oh right, maybe this isn't over yet, he still wants to spend time with me, and suddenly I'm very happy again.

Then we walk to this diner nearby, which I really like because it's so American and quaint and the menu has things like "silver dollar pancakes" and "Aunt Jennie's corned beef hash and eggs" and it's open twenty-four hours and has a waiter called Doug who's a clear recovering meth addict and has lovely glazed blue eyes and I order some food for myself at the counter and pay, and then Lloyd walks up to me and touches my shoulder affectionately and looks into my eyes and asks:

"Can you get my food as well?"

"Why?"

"You know I don't have any money right now."

"Not even money to feed yourself?"

"Well, no."

"That's too bad, but now that you've broken up with me, I don't think I'm responsible for feeding you anymore."

Then he gets really mad at me and storms out of the diner and I have to sit there and eat my Idaho rainbow trout burger all alone.

On Friday night I sit by the pool at my dad's place and

don't contact Lloyd at all, but instead I go through his Face-book and look at all his friends and send friend requests to everyone who's male, American, aged eighteen to thirty-eight and at least a six out of ten in terms of appearance, and there's about two thousand profiles that fit that description. That boy has a lot of friends and they're all over the country and I'm sure that he doesn't know them, but they must serve a purpose in contributing hundreds of likes every time that he posts some-thing, not to mention the relentless exchange of flirtatious messages and naked as well as seminaked selfies via inbox. Up to this point and in my whole Facebook career I mostly added friends that I knew in real life with very few exceptions, but where has that gotten me? Single at thirty-four next to my dad's pool on a Friday night in January, that's where. While Lloyd's technique of indiscriminate adding (which is how he also approached me initially) has gotten him staying in a beach apartment in Venice, California, for free and having big nights out partying in West Hollywood, again for free. One of us seems to be doing it right.

All these other men in need of attention around the coun-try start responding by accepting my friend requests (I have changed my profile picture to a shirtless beach one), and this appears to have a cumulative effect, as I suddenly also start receiving hundreds of friend requests because I start showing up on people's timelines as having become friends with their friends.

On Saturday daytime I still refrain from contacting Lloyd directly, and only around 9:00 P.M. do I message him and ask how he's doing. He replies about an hour later saying that he's hanging out with his friends in WeHo but it's not going to be a late night, because he doesn't like going out on the scene, as I know. Around 1:30 A.M. he gets tagged in a picture at Here bar on Instagram and between 1:30 A.M. and 3:00 A.M. he ignores about thirty-five calls from me, even though his WhatsApp and Facebook Messenger show to me that he's active on his phone. Eventually he turns his phone off.

On Sunday after 12:30 P.M. he messages me and asks me why I've sent friend requests to all his friends on Facebook and I reply with the question how he was able to go out and get drunk again, if he didn't have money to buy himself some scrambled eggs the day before and I was being asked to pay for his food. He doesn't reply and we don't interact anymore, not even when I get home early on Sunday evening and find him passed out on the couch in the living room.

35

I have never felt as nostalgic for Germany as I do currently, not ever in my life. Ever since I traveled to England when I was twelve and decided that I wanted to be English, and then especially from the age of sixteen, when I actually moved there, I've held Germany in mild disdain. Now I'm constantly watching German TV shows from the 1990s on YouTube and listening to German pop songs, again from when I was young, which I had previously turned my nose up at. For the first time in my life also, I am missing my mum. This has never happened to me before. I guess it took eighteen years.

This afternoon I ride my bike to the post office, pick up a postcard, write on it, "Don't think that I never miss you," and send it to her. This will come as a shock, I'm sure, from a child who can never say "I love you" back every time she says it because it feels way too intimate. For that reason alone I phrased my message with two negatives ("don't think," "never miss") so that the end result is a positive message, but not one that you don't have to work around the sentence logically to figure out.

36

On Sunday afternoon I am looking for revenge sex on Grindr.

The guy I was just dating and who's still staying at my house and refused to sleep with me throughout my "relationship" for reasons that he will never explain and I will never understand, the same guy who flipped out on me the first time that I met him because I admitted to having used dating apps in the past, does not recognize my headless torso picture because he's an idiot and he sends me a message on Grindr, the app that he has previously claimed he has never used because it's disgusting to him, and the message says:

"Into?"

Lloyd also has a headless torso on his profile, but I guess I'm not an idiot, plus I can clearly see my bathroom in the background of the picture where he took it, so I know that it's him. And I write back:

"Lots. You?"

I'm at home and he's somewhere that I don't know, but it's six miles away according to Grindr. By the time that I've seen his message and written back he's gone offline, so he doesn't reply. At this point I take four Xanax and go for a walk down on the beach.

I come home in the evening and have dinner. Lloyd is still out. I watch some TV in the living room and eventually go into my bedroom to go to sleep. Around half past midnight I hear him come in. He uses the bathroom and from what I can hear goes and lies on the sofa to sleep. I grab my phone and put Grindr on. He's online and he's messaged me back. He still hasn't figured out that it's me.

He says that he likes my picture and asks for some more. I freak out a little bit because I want to keep talking to him to figure out what he wants, how far he would take it with a stranger on Grindr, so I can't tell him that he's talking to me yet. I quickly go on Facebook and steal the pictures of some gay guy I know in London whose body is similar to mine. I send Lloyd pictures of the London guy and Lloyd sends me back some of himself. He tells me that he "literally loves fucking and getting fucked." I say that he seems to be pretty close and ask whether he wants to meet now. He finally starts getting suspicious and asks me exactly where I am. I give him an address that's three blocks away. He points out that I seem to be the closest person to him according to the app and doesn't believe me. A couple of minutes later, he blocks me.

I storm out of my bedroom and we shout at each other for a bit. I tell him that he's a hypocrite and a liar and he calls me a creep, trying to trick him by messaging him using a fake profile and fake pictures. I remind him that he messaged me first without recognizing me, like a moron, and ask him to move out of my place first thing tomorrow. He says that he'll move out when he has the money to do so and tells me that I'm fucking crazy and I should leave him alone, and then I go back to bed and snort three Zopiclone before passing out.

The pills must really have worked, because the next morning I wake up at eleven thirty. Lloyd is still lying on the couch. I go sit at the computer and check Facebook to see whom he's added and what pictures he's liked, but realize that he's removed me and blocked me from his friends.

I turn around to face him and ask him if he's fucking kidding me. He scrunches up his face because I used a "cuss word" and I'm therefore immoral and says that, yes, he deleted me and he doesn't want to have anything to do with me anymore. I remind him that he's still living in my apartment for free and that I'm paying for all his food.

We continue arguing and it quickly escalates. The main point of my arguing is that he's an unemployable loser and he needs to get the hell out of my space. The main point of his arguing is that I'm a psychopathic stalker who's obsessed with him. In essence, we are both making extremely valid points.

I am getting more and more aggravated and he's playing it quite cool, but that's mainly because I have feelings for him and he doesn't care about me at all. It's very easy not to lose your temper if you're emotionally uninvolved.

At one point, as I'm shouting at him repeatedly to get out

of my house, he takes his phone out and starts recording our argument. I ask him what he's doing and he says that I'm being really hilarious and he wants to play back the argument later to his friends, so they can all see how crazy I am.

I leap forward and try to grab his phone and stop him from recording. He pulls back. As we both scramble for the phone, we fall on the floor and start screaming and punching each other. Somebody starts knocking on my front door and I get up to answer it. The building manager is here to tell me that the neighbors are complaining about the noise. "Can you settle down?" he asks. He doesn't want to have to call the police. I apologize and say that we'll stop right now.

I go back in the living room and continue arguing with Lloyd, only in a quieter voice and sitting down on the sofa. This lasts about fifteen seconds before we start shouting again. This time I take my phone out and call Peter while holding it up in the air. Lloyd asks me what I think I'm doing. I say that if he wants to have evidence of our fight, so do I. I can't quite hear what's happening on my phone, because we're both too loud and I'm not holding it next to my ear, but at this point either Peter has answered and is listening, trying to figure out what's going on, or it has gone to voice mail and it's recording. Lloyd doesn't make an effort to grab my phone or stop me from recording like I did. Instead, he starts yelling that I should step back from him and leave him alone and that I'm really scaring him right now. I'm quite startled because this doesn't make sense, we're both sitting down, and all I can do is ask him what he's talking about, quite incredulously, and point out that I couldn't intimidate him physically anyway because he's much taller than me and weighs fifty pounds more. He then shouts, "Put the knife down," (there is no knife, clearly) and I don't even know what's happening anymore, but I think he's just won.

37

Yesterday evening, three months after he moved in, two months after we broke up, and almost three weeks after our physical fight, Lloyd finally moved out of my flat.

I wake up early on Thursday morning to use the bathroom and this is the first time in two months when I don't have to glance over at the living room sofa to check that he's sleeping there, because I know that he's not. Well, it's the first morning when I know for a fact that he won't be there, there's no need to check, and no anxiety comes with the fact that he's not. But I glance anyway. I go back to bed and take some more Ambien and some more Valium and start checking my phone for messages from different time zones. I think I fall asleep maybe a couple of hours later and wake up after 10:00 A.M., when I decide to get up.

I have nothing to do today apart from pack for my trip to Hawaii tomorrow morning.

I have breakfast—cereal from a blue bowl and a protein shake from a shaker, both of which we had bought together.

As he only moved out yesterday and as we have only lived in this apartment together and have acquired everything in it together, everything reminds me of him now that he's not here.

I decide to do some laundry, primarily for my trip, but also so I can wash the blanket that he used to sleep in on the sofa. It's a plaid blue and maroon blanket from Ralph Lauren that I bought a couple of years ago in London. I have no idea how a flimsy single blanket felt adequate for this enormously muscular man on a bare sofa for the two months that he slept there after he broke up with me. He packed up all his stuff when he left yesterday, but this was my blanket, so it stayed, and it's soaked with his scent.

I pick it up and wrap it all around me. I don't think he'll ever hug me again, but right now he encloses me. I fall on the floor with the blanket still around me and I jerk off in it with his smell pushed against my face, picturing fucking him hard on all fours. I then do the laundry, fighting thoughts to keep this blanket unwashed forever.

When I bring it back, I wrap it around me once again and lie on the floor. I take a picture of my head with only my eyes peeking out and post it on Instagram with the Cults' lyric "I knew right then that I'd been abducted."

I set off to go to the gym on my bike even though I'm feeling sick. Halfway through, I give up and return home.

38

On Saturday my main focus is to have sex with anyone on this planet. I am armed with GHB to get me high and horny and forget all the previous exes I'm moping about, and a number of Viagra tablets to assist with my emotionally caused impotence problem. I am not going to leave this flat until I manage to do this.

I'm texting Peter, and his advice is that I should change my Grindr profile headline to say, "Straight guy looking NOW," and then add some extra information about how I'm not gay, I have a girlfriend, I need to keep this on the down-low, etc., because that's really sexy to guys apparently and people will soon start forming a queue to sleep with me.

I go online, make the suggested edits, and talk to several people for a couple of hours until I find someone I like, who's willing to come over. This is somebody I've met before, actually, he's a friend of a friend of a friend of a friend and we went to the same concert once when he was visiting London a couple of years ago. I haven't seen him since and he doesn't seem to remember me. He doesn't live very far from me and says he'll be over in half an hour. I take a dose of G, one Viagra, put a record on, and start pacing around the flat, freaking the hell out.

The man arrives and rings my doorbell. He comes upstairs, I open the door, we exchange two sentences of extremely uncomfortable small talk and then start making out. About ten seconds into this, he pulls away and asks, "What did you say your name was?" I tell him my name and ask for his, even though I already know it. He tells me his name. It would seem that now he suddenly remembers me. He then says, "Oh sorry, bud, I forgot to put the parking permit in my car downstairs and I might get a ticket. Let me go do that right now." I ask if he actually needs a parking permit, because I have a spare one to give him, but he says no, he lives in the neighborhood, so he has one. He says he'll be back in two minutes. He leaves my flat. Twenty minutes later, it becomes obvious that he's never coming back. I check Grindr again and he's blocked me, so I can't message him to ask what the deal is.

I text Peter with everything that happened. He tells me to take another dose of G and keep trying. I take another dose of G, spend about half an hour talking to more people, then I get really tired, most likely because I took too much G, and I fall asleep on my sofa. I wake up about an hour later and check my messages. Within an hour, a twenty-two-year-old student who's just moved to LA has been to my place and we have fucked each other. The actual sex must have lasted about six minutes. It was a dreadful experience, but at least I am now sexually active again.

On Friday evening Peter comes over to Venice and we go out to eat. I am feeling particularly down, even by my own recent standards. When dinner is over, we go back home and take a couple of doses of a morphine-based painkiller that Peter has saved from last year when he was prescribed it after dislocating his shoulder. I have this idea that I want to take a bath and I want Peter to be there and watch me, but I don't want him to be able to touch me or be part of it in any other way. Peter agrees to that. I take my clothes off and get in the bath. Peter sits on a chair in the bathroom and watches, and then about twenty minutes later he says that he doesn't want to do this anymore and he goes home. And I just sit there. Soaking.

39

On Thursday night I finish some work and then walk down to the beach to watch the sunset by myself and listen to some music, but then I hurry back home before the sun has gone down because I remember I need to cut the sleeves off a shirt that I just bought before going to the gym tonight and this is making me lose concentration right now until it's finally and properly done.

At home, while I'm measuring fabric that's about to get cut, I receive a Facebook message from somebody I'm friends with but I don't know how and the message says:

"Sorry for the ambush ass vid. Had some wine and was feeling horny for you lol."

Then he attaches a video of himself sitting up on a sofa, spreading his legs, and jiggling his ass. It looks good.

I tell him that I saw a picture he posted today and that I thought he looks good, but the video is killing me and he's sexy as fuck. He then tells me that he wants to meet me so bad and asks if I ever go up to Oregon. I say no. We then go back and forth for a bit discussing meeting up for a sex weekend, either in LA or Oregon or somewhere in between, and we exchange a few more pictures and videos.

Then Anthony, whom I've started talking to again, texts me and he says:

"The hottest guys are at Pavilions right now, I am purposely driving around the parkin lot to see what cars they get into. Don't judge."

I write back:

"You are talking to a guy who's going to the gym tonight at eleven just to work out next to a hot guy who was there last night at the same time, who am I to judge?"

"One just got in a jeep."

"Very good."

Then I send Anthony the original ass video from the guy from Oregon and Anthony asks who that is and I say that it's a random Facebook guy who's drunk and sending me videos and wants to drive to LA to get fucked, and Anthony says that well, he's been to Oregon and he's seen what's there, so this makes total sense.

Then he texts me that the other hot guy got in an Audi and that we should go to grocery stores to cruise more often. I agree, cut my shirt so it's ready for the gym, wait around for a couple more hours doing nothing, and then set off to catch my gym crush at 11:00 P.M.

40

At the gym, there is a guy who's been genetically modified to appeal to sad gay men by being physically perfect. They have also dressed him head to toe in store-window, current season Nike apparel, and have given him a badass Mercedes to drive because they know we're all about the surface. I work out my legs and stare at him for the duration of my workout as he walks around with perfect posture, towering over everyone, performing robotically perfect back and shoulder exercises, his muscles bulging from every possible direction, hurting me inside. From his shin hair peeking underneath his calf-length Nike leggings and his square shoulders, to his cutthroat jawline and the stern look in his eyes, he is perfect. I am using all my strength not to run up to him sobbing and beg him to love me, or at least let me lick his sweaty armpit once and forget about me forever. Either will do.

Then I leave the gym and turn on Grindr, just on the off chance that he's gay. The gym robot isn't on it, but some other guy from the gym has messaged me. He is unattractive to me and therefore invisible. The invisible person, whom I genuinely don't remember seeing in the gym at all, has said:

"All the sexy guys at the gym at this time."

I don't want to admit that it was me that he saw yet (my profile has a headless torso picture) so I say:

"They are?? Who's there?"

"Were you at the gym?"

Then I give up, plus I want to talk about the gym robot, so I type:

"Sure I was. Which guys did you like?"

"Any pic?"

"Let's just talk about the other guys"

"Which one did u like," the invisible man asks me.

"I like the tall one with the shaved head who wears full Nike outfits all the time."

"He was wearing blue today huh?"

"Yes. What's his deal?"

"Yes I saw him. He's huge."

"I know. I'm in lust with him. Why does he walk around like that?"

"He knows he's good."

Then I type:

"You have to do something."

Then I type:

"You have to get him for me."

Then I type:

"I can't live like this anymore."

And then the invisible person stops responding to me, so I guess we are through.

41

On Thursday evening, Peter and I drive down to Indio, near Palm Springs, for Coachella. When the tickets went on sale a few months ago I bought two, having planned to go with Lloyd, but then all that went to hell, so I gave my second ticket to Peter. There was never a chance that I wasn't going to go. Coachella combines everything I have ever loved about this world: alternative music, social posturing, and straight bros. I've been to five so far because I used to travel all the way from London to go after I discovered it. During Coachella weekend, I experience an elevated state of living, which, no matter what I do, I cannot re-create for the rest of the year. In the other fifty-one weekends of the year, I merely subsist.

We're staying at a house just half a mile away from the festival that Markus and Anthony have rented for the weekend. It's in one of those gated cul-de-sacs in the desert where a lot of middle-aged couples from Los Angeles keep houses for their retirement. You can tell this by the decor, which brings together brass, geometric mirrors, flowery lamp shades, and pastels in combinations last seen in Angela Lansbury's house in *Murder, She Wrote*. The antiquated interior is counteracted by a number of young people who are having very modern fun times indeed. When we get there after 10:00 P.M. a bit of a party is under way. This turns out to be a typical LA party with the exact same people you'd find in a Hills mansion on any given Friday night, simply transported a hundred miles southeast.

I have a couple of lines of coke and a few tequila shots that people force into me, but just a couple of hours later I take some Ambien and fall asleep in the bedroom that I'm assigned, because I want to be rested for the actual weekend. There is a certain cleverness to the idea of arriving somewhere early, starting to drink/take drugs early, collapsing early, and leaving early, but really, people need to learn to pace themselves for a three-day-long music festival.

On Day 1, I watch four or five bands that I'm half-interested in and a big-name DJ that I'm not interested in at all, but all my friends are, along with the majority of the dumbest, hottest straight guys at the festival. I take a lot of GHB and ketamine, and find a bag with twelve pills that someone's dropped on the ground somewhere. I split them among my friends, and they're really good. I overhear a guy telling his friend, "I need a chick, dude" while we're all standing at the urinals trying very hard to pee although the drugs are making it very difficult, and momentarily feel sorry for straight guys, who seem to have to make an effort to get a girl, even in an environment like this where everyone is high and easy to talk to. I lose my shirt, of course, which was tucked into the waistband of my shorts from the moment I walked into the festival. And I make out for a really, really long time on the dance floor of the Do

LaB stage with a tall, blond navy guy who's based in San Diego and I have previously known only via Instagram.

On Day 2, I re-create looks that I've stolen from straight guys that I saw walking around on Day 1, including taking my shirt and tying it around my head like a headband, because I want to belong. I become acquainted with random festival-goers, exchange drugs with them, roll around on grassy fields with old and new friends, and take pictures that nobody will want to see in the morning. When it gets really windy in the evening, I buy a Coachella hoodie to keep warm and tie my shirt around my face, completely covering my mouth and nose so that I don't breathe in the desert sand that's flying around everywhere. Everyone is doing this. At one point, I leave everyone that I know and everyone that I've just met and go by myself to see Suede, my favorite band of all time, who broke up after I was twenty and recently reunited. I spend half the set crying because it's so good and because I remember what it was like being sixteen again. I go back and find everyone that I know, Peter, Anthony, Markus, Rus, Daniel, X, a dozen other guys from LA, dancing in the DJ tent and taking turns making out with one another, and I join them.

On Day 3, I start taking drugs at 11:00 A.M. because it's the last day. I accidentally fall in a k-hole by early afternoon and regret it, because I end up missing two bands I really wanted to see. Late in the evening, I meet a guy while queuing up to buy ice cream (it's the only thing I can swallow) who complains to me, "I've had so much coke, man. I've lost my sense of smell." I ask him, "Is there another sense that's heightened, as a result?" He says, "Yes, my sense of self," and he takes off his shirt, then raises his arms and flexes his biceps. I find

this charming and I start making out with him. We go to the
bathroom together and when we walk in, we see a really drunk
straight guy standing there, stroking his dick. He glances at
us, then his dick, like we're gonna walk over and help him, and
I'm not going to pretend that I'm above that, but he's not hot at
all so we pass. We walk into a cubicle and the guy with no
sense of smell gets on his knees and starts going down on me.
I take my phone out and start filming him until he looks up,
shakes his head no, and continues. He wants to leave the
festival early and go home to fuck, but I say I can't do that and
go find Peter and all the others and dance with them until the
music stops.

42

On Wednesday I start my day successfully by waking up.

Today I'm lucky enough that a bro meme appears as soon as I open Facebook and scroll through my timeline. A few pop news websites have picked up a story that appeared on last night's MTV reality show *True Life* about a twenty-two-year-old college baseball bro whose biggest problem in life is his giant butt. A short clip of the show has been reposted around, where he complains that no one takes him seriously. That he goes out and feels objectified. That he's worried his career will suffer (he's graduating this year) because in any office he works in, the ass will be the distraction that will overshadow his achievements. All this complaining is delightfully interspersed with shots of him going up and down stairs, tearing through pairs of trousers, waddling into college parties, and swinging baseball bats with his, objectively, enormous butt.

All the elements of this story are making me short-circuit. There is an all-American athletic bro. He plays college baseball. He is tall, blue-eyed, and he has an unnaturally big butt. He is tortured and he needs help. My help. This is all too much. I need to track him down.

I spend a good half hour replaying the short clip from Facebook with the highlights of the show and reading the comments that other desperate gays such as myself have left on the news sites that reported this. I then find the actual show online on MTV and watch it twice. Following that, and now in a complete frenzy because nowhere is there a mention of his surname, we only get a reference to his stupid generic first name ("Luke"), and I can't find him online. I start going mental on Google. I google the TV show. I google the state where he lives and his name. I google his sister's first name (she also appeared on the show to provide moral support), in conjunction with his name and the state where they live. Nothing. Then I go back and watch the show a third time and try to find a name for the college that he attends. They are too smart and they haven't given it. Then as I watch his beautiful dumb sad eyes nearly in tears once again because a girl shouted "dat ass" as he walked past her last night, I have an epiphany. He plays baseball, doesn't he? I go on Google and search for all the college baseball teams that exist in his state. Do you know how many Lukes play college baseball in Kentucky? Many. But I have plenty of time and all the patience in the world and I finally find him. I now have a few more pictures, his height (six two), weight (210 pounds), and a lovely little blurb about what he likes to do in his spare time. I look him up on Facebook, Twitter, and Instagram and follow him on all three.

Then it's suddenly late afternoon and I walk to Whole Foods to buy some lunch, because I've forgotten to eat today.

43

A couple of days ago, I messaged Lloyd on Gchat. I really want to see him and talk to him about something. He took his time but eventually he got back to me and I forced a brief conversation out of him and then asked if he wanted to have coffee sometime. He said yes, so I suggested this Friday. We're supposed to meet tonight.

I call him up to set up a time and decide on a place and he even answers on my third attempt (even though I'm also checking his Scruff profile at the same time, and he is constantly online there, which means that he's holding his phone in his hand but just deciding to ignore my first couple of calls) and suggests that we go to a coffee shop in West Hollywood. I say fine and ask if he wants me to pick him up instead of both of us driving there and trying to find parking, and he says, no, he'll drive himself there, thank you very much. I say that this doesn't make sense and I think that he just doesn't want me to know where he lives and he says that's damn right he doesn't want me to know where he lives. I ask him why and he says because it's his life and he doesn't want his ex-boyfriend to know where he lives. I tell him that this is really offensive and remind him that he stayed at my place for three months for free and he still owes me a lot of cash on top of that if he really needs to hear it, and in any case we are friends now and any normal person wouldn't have a problem telling his friends where he lives. He tells me that he agreed to have coffee to-night at a real push, but since I'm acting like this I can forget about it and hangs up on me. This really freaks me out and I call him right back and my eyes are getting wet and he picks up and I apologize for being so irrational as to wanting to know where he lives and say that of course we can meet at the coffee shop and we agree to meet at 8:00 P.M. We hang up and I already hate both him and myself more than I did half an hour ago and who would have thought this would even be possible.

After this I spend a little time staring at a wall, obsessing about my loneliness and thinking what time I should go to the gym, until I receive a poke and an inbox message on Facebook. They are both from a gentleman called Seth Ryder and the message reads:

"I'm not sure what the definition of a poke is, but I did it, and there's no turning back"

Now, I don't know Seth in real life, but it turns out that he follows me on Instagram and he has a very hot boyfriend that I'm definitely very interested in, so I assume that in order to get to the boyfriend, I have to talk to Seth first. Both Seth and his boyfriend appear to live in Chicago. I write back:

"I'm learning about pokes as I go along, just like you, but this was certainly not objectionable. How's it going?"

Then we make some small talk, how the week is treating us, where we are from, what we do, until I finally ask him if he has a boyfriend.

Seth: Yes, I do. He's in law school and lives in a different city right now.

Me: How far is this different city? Long-distance can be hard.

Seth: About 3 hours away. We've got it down though so it's not too bad. And anyway, we may be together but we're not dead. Ha

Me: I'm trying to read between the lines in what you just said, but I'm too stupid. Please rephrase?

Seth: My bad. I think a lot of people have preconceived notions of what a relationship is or should be and that we operate more under the assumption that what works for us may not work for everybody. We're together but not dead to the world as individuals.

Me: I think you're implying that you are free to sleep with other people. Is this correct?

Seth: You've seen right through me. This is partially true. There are rare occasions where another person is involved, but that's something we do together.

Me: Got it. Everything is clear now. You sometimes have threesomes, and you would like me to be part of that.

Seth: Maybe I should have just come out and said that.

Me: Said what?

Seth: Hi, I'm Seth. I sometimes have 3somes with my boyfriend and we want to have one with you.

Me: Hi, I'm Konrad. I sometimes take part in 3somes as
a third, and I would like to have one with you and
your boyfriend.

Seth: Well, I'm glad we got that established. I guess I can
give up playing shy and just say flattering things to
you.

Me: You don't have to say flattering things, but you can
give up playing shy for sure.

Seth: Perfect. So what does it take to get my hands on
you?

At this point I screenshot the conversation and send it to
Peter, along with the Instagram profile links for Seth and his
boyfriend. Then I reply to Seth.

Me: Well, I suppose distance is a one really prohibitive
factor at the moment

Seth: That's easily taken care of. Just know that I'd really
like to. Get my hands on you. Or rather we'd like to.

At this point this is really turning me on because it's such a
Lloyd scenario: talking to some couple in another city, being
flirty as fuck, getting them to fly you out there for a sex weekend. And seeing that Lloyd is my current obsession and I want
to emulate everything that he does, well, I'm really into this.
So I continue with Seth.

Me: This sounds very good to me. So am I visiting
Chicago?

Seth: Yeah! I'm all for that. You're welcome anytime.

Then I also screenshot this to Peter and add, "Why is he not offering to fly me out yet," and Peter writes back, "I guess you're good, but not that good," and then I leave the conversation with Seth because I assume I have to play hard to get a little bit at least, and then the flight offer will come in the next few days. (In the next few days, the flight offer does not come, but we do exchange some nudes via Snapchat.)

In the evening when it's time to go meet Lloyd I drive over to WeHo, park, and wait for him inside the coffee shop. My phone is showing a note, where I've written down what I want to say.

We broke up three months ago now, or we were never together, depending on what one's definition of a relationship is. In my heart there's hope for a reunion. My brain, however, says that my heart is a fucking idiot.

Lloyd shows up twenty minutes late and sits opposite me. He makes casual conversation for about ten minutes and of course that's very easy for him, because this meeting doesn't hold the same life-threatening importance that it's holding for me.

Once he's done, I deliver my speech almost straight from my phone's notes,

"I know you don't want to have a serious talk, but I need to get this off my chest. It's been clear from the last few months that you're not in love with me. You don't have romantic feelings for me. But I have these feelings for you. And that's fine. But I need to look out for myself. I need to know. Tell me that you don't have any feelings for me. Tell me that you don't now, and that you never will. I need you to set me free. Let me off the hook, so I can move on."

Then Lloyd sets me free.

He leaves the coffee shop in a huff when I ask him, please, not to contact me in any way for the foreseeable future and I also get up and go seconds later to avoid the stare from the middle-aged writer at the next table who has overheard the entire conversation.

I drive back home, where I don't feel anything for approximately four hours.

44

On Sunday morning I wake up and go to the gym and then the beach and I'm sure I was supposed to also work for a bit because my dad has been complaining that I'm not putting in as many hours as he would like me to, but suddenly it's 8:00 P.M. and I've completely run out of time and a masc musc bro from Grindr is about to come over. Yes, this masc musc bro is six two and yes, he's studying at the moment and working part-time as a model and yes, he's got all the muscles that you want him to have, but primarily the reason why I want it so bad is that his blurb on Grindr is that he refuses to accept messages from anyone who has a visible face on their profile picture because those people are out and shameless and clearly nonmasc enough. This means that he has gigantic issues about his sexuality, is self-hating to the nth degree, and his internalized homophobia might just be surpassing mine. Add to that the fact that some of his messages to me have included "aight bro," "yo," "right on," "down to wait," "for sure bro," "solid," "I'm horny bro," and "leaving in 10 bro," and I have no choice but to collapse into a heap and meet this guy.

The word "discreet" is by far the most commonly used description in Grindr bios, with the only competition coming from the number of people who state "neg4neg" and type in the date of when they were last tested and found "clean."

Then my guy turns up in a large SUV and I go outside to hand him a permit so he can park on my street. I walk up to his car, he opens his window, and I attempt some small talk. He grunts a couple of times and drives off to find a parking spot. I sit down on the steps outside my building to wait for him, and he only comes back around ten minutes later, by which point I have started to think that he took one look at me, changed his mind, and drove off. Also stealing my permit.

But even now, upstairs in my apartment, he's completely masc musc and gives one-word answers, and even those are so mumbled to the point where I think that he might be mentally impaired, and he doesn't smile even for a second or show any human emotion that might indicate he wants to be there, and I don't even know that he's into me or completely repulsed and is still trying to make a quick escape, until his tongue is in my mouth and our baseball caps are clashing against each other. Then we have sex, and I can objectively rate this as a 5.4/10 experience, one that was a lot better in my head before he turned up.

Then the awkward time comes when I have to walk him to

his car so I can pick up my permit, and those few minutes are
spent making stilted conversation where I ask him questions
about himself, where he grew up, what he's studying, and he's
coming up with lies for each one while looking extremely
uncomfortable, because, I don't know, I'll track down his
parents, run straight to them, and tell them that their son is
gay? Something like that.

When I get back home, I jerk off and cum once again,
because I'm still hard from the Viagra I took to get through
this. Then Peter starts texting me drunk from a work colleague's gay wedding where he's gone tonight in a town called
Ojai, northwest of Los Angeles.

Peter: I'm now walking 1.4 miles back to the hotel
        because there are no cabs here.
Me: Can't one of the drunk guests drive you?
Peter: We were lured to a pool party that never hap-
        pened.
Me: Those fucking gays.
Peter: Exactly!
Peter: I got really drunk and told everyone about sleep-
        ing with [well known gay singer Peter has slept with]
Me: That's nice.
Peter: I then pleaded with everyone to tell me something
        more shameful.
Peter: And my boss said he likes to piss on guys.
Me: You kill me.
Peter: Which of course made me OBSESSED with my
        boss.

Peter: I MUST HAVE HIS PISS.

Me: Ask for a urine sample. Or does it have to stream directly for you to be happy?

Peter: I will not be satisfied until my boss pees on me. What happens after that is none of my concern.

Peter: This is all very real.

Peter: Should I sleep with my boss?

Me: Yeah man, why not?

Peter: Orrrr . . . should I want to sleep with him and become obsessed?

Me: The latter. 100% the latter.

Peter: Really????? I grabbed his back sexually several times.

Me: Yeah really. Imagine the drama, the intrigue, the plotting, the heightened emotions.

Peter: Fine. He now knows that another daddy fucked me repeatedly and I know that he pissed on guys several times. But we will just go on with our business as usual.

Me: That's better than doing anything with him. If you do anything with him, it will become boring. This is intense.

Peter: That's true. Thank you.

The conversation ends and I decide to text the closeted guy from earlier and tell him that I had a really good time, not because I actually did, but because I want him to respond and say the same thing to me, because I can't stand knowing that he possibly didn't like me, so I write:

"That was fun, dude."

He writes back, "It was for sure," one hour and ten minutes later, which indicates that he doesn't think it was fun at all either, and then I go to bed.

45

On Thursday morning I wake up and I'm reading the news, because I thought of this new concept where sometimes you have to be less insular and self-absorbed and maybe look at the world around you and realize that other people have problems too and you're not the center of the fucking universe. I guess it's worth trying.

I'm reading news from Europe, and particularly this story that broke in Greece last week about a kid in some small town up north who went missing about a month ago. He was twenty. So he went missing and they were trying to find him for several weeks, and the things that came out while they were trying to find him were that he used to be bullied really badly and the code words that were used for the reasons why he was bullied were that he "wasn't masculine enough" and he was "too quiet" and he didn't live up to the "manly" ideals that a twenty-year-old guy should live up to, behaviorally. Then last week he was found dead. It's not yet known whether someone killed him or whether he killed himself, but I believe the narrative doesn't change that much either way.

When they found this kid dead, there was an uproar in Greece and everyone stood up for him on TV and on the Internet, which are the places that matter now, and of course there were some oddball idiots who wrote things against him still, but they were just a small minority that was quickly dismissed. And everyone's uproar concerned "bullying," and everyone was up in arms about this phenomenon and wanted it to stop. Right now. The fact that the kid was implied to be gay and that's why he was bullied is not something that's said out loud, because even now, with incidents like this, it's not something that can be brought up explicitly in some societies, and even the biggest supporters of Vaggelis, because that's the kid's name, are not fighting a fight for gay acceptance, they are fighting a fight for those men who are "not masculine enough," or "too quiet." But it's fine. Societies advance at their own pace and for now in Greece they're going to have to use codes.

And then, with all that, I thought, well, what the hell am I doing as a grown, out gay man spending all my time pretending to be straight with all my baseball caps and basketball shorts, especially now that I'm living in America. How am I helping anyone to feel more comfortable if they're insecure, if they're scared to come out? What is my message? Are they only going to be accepted, is their only hope to stay alive, first literally and then metaphorically, if they act more straight than the straight dudes?

I think about masculinity a lot and what it means and how it's qualified against being a homosexual male. This is an issue even outside the small towns of northern Greece. You may not be bullied explicitly for not being masculine in West Holly-wood in LA and Soho in London, but the predominant behavioral ideal right now is heteronormative. Via Sean Cody. Heteronormative males are what the majority of us jerk off to and what the majority of us want to be.

Not to mention, this obsession with masculinity and the dismissal of any alternative slips into the slang used by gay males. We often use female pronouns to talk dismissively about others when we want to degrade them, or even gently mock them. When you're mad at your friend and you text your other friend and say, "She's a bit crazy, that one," you attempt to di-minish them by taking away their masculinity.

Then there is the go-to gay slur from one gay male to another, of course, about being a bottom. Everyone is always fucking accused of being a bottom. Nobody uses the term "top" dismis-sively. Nobody leaves anonymous comments on websites accus-ing people of being tops. This takes us full circle, back to cultures where being a bottom equals being gay, but being a top means that you're just a guy who likes to fuck.

I don't know why the world thinks like that. I don't know why effeminate men are berated. Maybe the gay issue is ulti-mately a sexism one. As a grown gay man, I don't want young kids who are not out to be scared. I certainly don't want them to get bullied and disappear and kill themselves. But I also don't want them to think that they can only fit in by acting how society tells them to. Yet here I am, going to the gym every day in a backward baseball cap supporting a sports team that I've never seen play.

46

On Tuesday I aim to get up really early and go get my hair cut, because the later you go, the longer you have to wait. I manage to wake up and make it to the barbershop at ten thirty, which is not early, not early at all, and there are about eight people ahead of me. Potentially you can call up in advance and make an appointment, but I don't make phone calls and talk to somebody that's not immediate family or a current boyfriend, so that's just not going to happen.

I used to cut my own hair in my twenties, but then I was suddenly thirty-four and I had lost my youth and could use all the help I could get, so I decided to have it done by someone who knows what they're doing. Well. Twenty-five dollars' worth of knowing what they're doing. So I have my hair cut one week, then it looks good for a week or ten days after that and then it starts looking awful, so I start wearing a hat constantly for three weeks, and then I have my hair cut again.

My barbershop is run by a group of no-nonsense straight Latino bros. They talk endlessly about baseball, breasts, and other blue-collar topics that I don't understand. The person who cuts my hair is my favorite, because he never attempts to start a conversation with me. I suspect that's because he knows I'm foreign and don't follow the Dodgers, and what the hell would he have to talk to me about? He's also my favorite because he's quiet overall, compared to the others. I also like going there because I'm an ethnic minority and it always feels like the beginning of those porn scenes where a clueless white guy walks into a garage full of tattooed, ethnically diverse meatheads after his car has broken down in the middle of the desert and they proceed to gang-rape him, not that I want this to actually play through.

This Tuesday morning the barbershop TV is playing the 1977 bodybuilding documentary *Pumping Iron*, starring Arnold Schwarzenegger. The gumball candy machine they keep near the entrance next to the jar full of pennies is empty (who eats those? I wonder). And they have finally moved the naked pinup calendar hanging on the wall from the month of February (where it was all through February, March, and April) to November, arbitrarily. Maybe there weren't any hot girls during the spring and summer months. The most important conversation that takes place is the following:

> Young customer: I need to have my hair cut because I'm going to a wedding.
> Head barber: Oh yeah? Who you going with?
> Customer: On my own probably.
> Head barber: But who are you leaving with?
> Customer: The baddest one there.
> Head barber: So you want the "going to a wedding on

my own, but leaving with the baddest one there"
haircut?"

Customer: Yessir.

Head barber: Dis what I do.

Mateo finishes my haircut, gives me a voucher for three free
boxing classes, which I take both as a compliment and an in-
sult; I pay him and leave.

From there I drive to Beverly Hills to have an MRI scan on
my wrist, which has been hurting me for four weeks now ever
since I fell off my bike and landed on it. I went to the hospital
as soon as it happened and had an X-ray and it wasn't broken
and I've been wearing a brace to support it since, but the pain
hasn't gone away, and obviously I couldn't give it a rest and
stop working out, because what would I be without the gym,
the source of all of my confidence and my only social outlet
most days, but here I am a month later, still in pain, so I have
to have it checked out.

I check in with Maria and Brittany in reception and they
take me to a room where I can put all my stuff in a locker and
wait. Then Jimmy, the MRI technician, comes in and tells me
that it won't be much longer now, maybe eight more minutes,
and I'm fine with that to be honest, and then suddenly Jimmy
asks me if I'm going to the game later and it takes two seconds
of him pointing at my head for me to remember that I put on
an LA Dodgers cap that I found in my car after my haircut
because I didn't want small hairs to keep falling on my face
and neck. I laugh awkwardly and say, no, but it's already too
late and Jimmy has taken me for a big sports fan and is now
talking about a conflicting schedule this evening with the

Lakers. I'm thinking, honestly, Jimmy, can you not hear me speak? What Dodgers? What Lakers? What are you talking about?

Then Jimmy goes away, and what might have been a nice, boring eight-minute lull with me watching CNN on the small TV near the ceiling and flicking through half-year-old copies of *People* magazine has now become an agonizing countdown before Jimmy returns with more incomprehensible *SportsCenter* talk that I will have to navigate.

The terror of Jimmy returns in eleven minutes and twenty-three seconds (yes, I set the stopwatch on my phone after he left to count the sweet minutes of loneliness), and takes me to the next room, where he has to do some paperwork about my case and ask me the very important question:

"So is baseball your favorite sport then?"

Then I mumble something about soccer and being European and that sets him off on a very fervent dialogue (monologue) about the World Cup and all the different countries that prefer different sports and about sports video games and the most popular sports video game in the world being one about soccer, not about the NBA, as one might have guessed, and European people he used to work with who were also really into soccer and an old colleague who was also from England who ended up falling back on the bathtub and hitting his head on the bathtub and dying and he thinks he was actually drunk, but hey, it could happen to anyone, can I honestly tell him that I don't have a drink every once in a while, we all do, though he actually suspects that the English colleague who died was having a lot of problems with his wife and this is what drove him to drink so much and led to his subsequent fatal accident and, oh man, the food in England really sucks, every time they have a potluck here in the hospital the English girl who works in X-ray brings something nasty and, tell you what, those Italians have the best food, judging by Maria in reception's potluck contributions and he should set me up with her if I'm ever going to eat any decent food, or, hey, actually do I already have a girlfriend?

And after all this sports and bitches talk I just don't have it in my heart to disappoint him and tell him I'm gay and say, yes, yes, I have a girlfriend indeed. "Ah good deal, man," Jimmy says, drops a pair of headphones around my ears, and shoves me into the MRI machine, where I proceed to lay still and hear some loud throbbing noises for the next half an hour or so, only marginally obscured by the best hits of the 1980s, 1990s, and today, as played by DJ Shotgun on a local radio station that I don't recognize.

47

This weekend I'm going to San Francisco because I've really missed walking around in the summertime in thick London fog wishing I were someplace else, plus I have my friends Willa and Chris there who I want to see. On Friday afternoon my flight is scheduled for two, but there has never been an airplane that flew between Los Angeles and San Francisco that wasn't delayed, so I track the status of my flight online, and leave home two hours after the original time. Then, by the time I get to the airport and my gate, I discover that they have moved the flight forward by half an hour again, so, naturally, I've missed it. I sit there for a bit, considering whether this is really worth it, whether I really want to go, but the alternative of walking out of that airport, getting a taxi, and going back to Venice, which would take an hour, is too much to handle right now, so I talk to a bored airline person and get moved onto the next flight.

On the way to the next gate I stop at the bathroom and jerk off over the picture of a Hungarian wrestler that someone texted me as part of a BuzzFeed article called "Thighceps Are the New Biceps," about big legs now being more important than having a built upper body, and then I sit on the floor against a wall, because I think this makes me seem a lot cooler than sitting on a chair, and read my book while I wait.

As the people gather around waiting to board, there are two men who stand out. One of them is tall and muscular and he's wearing a tight shirt with very short sleeves, which are showing off his biceps, and tight unfashionable jeans. His face is acceptable, although without the body he would be a definite no. The other guy is also tall, maybe even slightly taller than the first one at a suspected six three, and he's also big, but his body is a lot softer and he's not wearing clothes to highlight it. His face is more handsome and less Mediterranean, and I guess I'm very mature this Friday afternoon, because in the competition I have started in my head about which guy is hotter, the guy with the worse body and better face wins.

Then we all get on the flight and like it only happens in books with underdeveloped storylines and pornographic films, I am sitting right next to the tall, handsome guy. Then the tall, handsome guy asks me what one of my tattoos means, and from that point on, over the course of the next forty-five minutes or however long the flight to San Francisco lasts, everyone around us enjoys a very intimate and embarrassing conversation where we each find out what the other person does, where he lives, where he's going to, where he works out (of course), what siblings he has, and which hand he jerks off with. After we've landed, we walk out toward the exit together, he asks for my number, and I give it to him.

Minutes after we go our separate ways, he sends me the following text:

"Hi, it's Justin. Thanks for the number. It was nice sitting next to you. This whole thing was a very pleasant surprise. I'd like to hang out with you again."

I write back:

"Hey. It was great meeting you. Would love to hang out. Enjoy your stay in SF."

The oddest thing about all this, of course, is that this is an attractive gay guy around my age who lives in Los Angeles that I've never come across before. In fact, it seems almost impossible. But, you know, I have found love on the plane and I'm not going to question it any further.

Then I decide to question it a little bit further, so I text Peter, who has lived in LA much longer than I have, and ask him if he knows of a guy called Justin, who works for a bank, is in his late thirties, originally from San Diego, and lives in Hollywood. Then twenty minutes later and having confirmed that this is the correct guy via comparing the phone number we both have for him, I have found out that Peter has already slept with him, that he is a loon, his body is unsalvageable, and he has some very weird fetishes. Then Justin starts texting me, asking if I'm free to hang while we're in San Francisco and also that he wants to devour my ass and dominate me in his hotel room either this evening or tomorrow evening, whichever works for me best, and then I haven't found love anymore and I stop responding.

In San Francisco some things happen and none of those things are important, and then it's Sunday afternoon and I'm at the airport again catching my flight back to LA. This is not a flight that Justin is on, and I am very thankful for that, so instead I have the pleasure of sitting next to a middle-aged lady, possibly in her early fifties, whose overly applied mascara and youthful knee-high boots imply that she is a recent divor-cée starved for romance. The bouquet of flowers she is parad-ing around like a trophy indicates that she's just found it.

Then, as we wait on the runway to take off, she gets her phone out and types the following message to a contact saved as "Nick [heart emoji] Weller" and I momentarily think that I'm sitting next to a preteen girl on Tumblr, apart from the fact that she writes it in all caps and she uses her right index finger to type slowly while holding the phone with her left hand far away from her face, which confirms that she is, in fact, in her fifties:

"I DON'T HAVE WORDS TO EXPRESS WHAT I FEEL MAYBE BECAUSE I THINK THAT WHAT WE HAVE IS SO SO SO SO SPECIAL"

Then she follows that up with:

"Sorry"

Nick [heart emoji] Weller doesn't feel that she needs to apologize because he feels the same way and they go back and forth like that for a bit, like drunk puppies, and then we are practically racing down the runway and she texts:

"I am yours."

He texts back:

"I am yours."

And then she turns her phone off and we shoot into the sky.

I could read my book during the flight, but I could also watch the love-struck divorcée go through her gallery of pic-tures with Nick from the weekend they've just spent together, and the latter is a lot more entertaining, so I do that. Dozens of pictures of an older gentleman with a thick gray mustache in a denim vest, the two together frolicking around a vineyard, then a deserted beach, all culminating in a series of selfies where they're making out while she steals glances at the camera, making sure they're both in the shot, so disturbing that I can't pull my eyes away.

Then eventually we land and she beats even me in turning her phone back on, where she immediately checks Facebook to see how the picture of them together she posted is doing (sunset, both smiling weatherworn smiles at the camera—a dignified shot at least and not one of the kissing ones) before she's even read the messages that he's sent while we were flying.

There's a lot of movement in the plane now as everyone is trying to get the hell out and I can't see her phone at all times, but I do catch a message where she types, "So kind, So tender, So strong, So everything," complete with funky punctuation and this is enough to lose faith in humanity now and forever. My phone buzzes and I see it's a text from Justin. I delete it without reading and block his number.

48

There's a restaurant in Venice that I provide as the answer to what my favorite restaurant in Venice is, but the last couple of times that I went there I was turned away because I was wearing a tank top and they said that they have a no-tank-tops rule, and I wasn't so sure that this was actually the case or they just didn't want me to be there. So on Friday afternoon I go online and check their website and find out that the dress code is real and they're not actually singling me out and refusing me entry. Then I go there and have dinner.

After dinner I walk down to the beach and between the hours of, say, ten thirty and twelve thirty I lie on a beach towel right next to lifeguard tower number 10, feet away from the ocean, in the dark, illuminated by only an iPhone screen going through a playlist that includes "Lemonade" by Sophie, "Novacane" by Frank Ocean, "Burning Up" by Madonna, "Fuck Up Some Commas" by Future, and "When Doves Cry" by Prince and, occasionally, by the blinding light the beach patrol is directing at me every time they drive by. There is absolutely nothing better to do on this planet.

On Saturday night I'm lying on my sofa watching Netflix and eating ice cream, practicing for Saturday nights over the next few decades, and then somebody knocks on my door. It's past 11:00 P.M.

I open the door in my underwear. It's Elvira from next door. She's holding a cup containing two bunches of an unidentified herb that's burning, producing a light, not unpleasant-smelling smoke. She tells me that it's sage and that it will help clear out evil spirits if I take it around my apartment. I ask whether I have to do this in every room and she says yes, I should do it now and I can bring the cup back to her when I'm done.

I take the cup with the burning herb and half close the door, because I'm not sure whether she wants to stand there and wait while I do this, or whether I have to go to her apartment when I'm done. She then walks away and I understand that I have to go next door to return it. I walk around with the cup in my living room and kitchen, then the fire has mostly gone out and there's hardly any smoke anymore, but I still take the cup to the bathroom and also walk into my bedroom, so that enough time has passed to prove that I actually did this when I go back.

I walk out and go next door. Her door is ajar. I knock lightly and return the cup to her. She talks to me a bit more about sage and asks me what I'm doing right now and tells me that I can always visit with her more, if I like. I tell her that right now I'm watching a film and I have to go back soon and she asks me what the film is. I tell her I'm watching *Rear Win-*

dow and she tells me she thought of Grace Kelly earlier today
and that her father once wrote a movie that Grace Kelly was
in. I am now standing in her living room, barefoot, still in my
underwear. She asks me if I smoke weed and I say no, and she
tells me a little bit about some projects that she's currently involved in, something to do with local government, some
proofreading stuff, some invites that she has to put together
for an event, etc. I ask if she knows who moved into the previously empty apartment opposite mine, and she says she thinks
it's an Asian girl, but she's not sure, she doesn't like to gossip
about the neighbors, but she did see a small androgynous person come out of the apartment recently and this androgynous
person was Asian and visiting the person who's just moved in,
and so yes, she thinks it's an Asian girl that moved in. I remind her of my film and she gives me one of the bunches of
sage to keep burning in my apartment if I like, then I leave, go
back, leave the burned-out sage on the kitchen counter, and go
lie on my sofa again and press play on *Rear Window*.

49

A group of us have come to Palm Springs because one of Peter's friends has a house there and he lets him use this house whenever he wants and we thought it might be a good idea to go there for the weekend. Peter is bringing three of his friends that I hardly know, and I'm bringing Hunter. Hunter is only twenty-two and he's my new best friend. He recently moved a few blocks away from me in Venice from Orange County, where he grew up. He's handsome, blond, inexperienced, and brand-new to the gay scene. And he's had the bad luck of immediately falling in with the wrong crowd, i.e., me.

Peter drove from LA with his friends on Friday, but I decided to stay the night and leave on Saturday, therefore committing to only one night's sleep in the Palm Springs house, because there are a total of six people staying there and I don't know what the sleeping arrangements are, how many rooms there are, how many beds, and that's very stressful to me.

When I get there with Hunter on Saturday at lunchtime all the others are tripping on mushrooms in the backyard around the pool and I don't feel like taking any hallucinogenics ever, so I suppose I'm glad I missed that. Four out of four guys on mushrooms are wearing baseball caps (two backward). Three out of four are wearing board shorts. One is just wearing a white towel tied around his waist, which he frequently removes to jump in the pool naked. They have a volleyball that they throw around and sometimes take breaks to do push-ups or flex their muscles for each other. Everyone is taking pictures of everything as it happens and posting them on Instagram. These guys have thousands of followers each and I dismiss the ones who have more followers than I do as "desperate" even though I'm just jealous.

Then Peter and his friends slowly come around from the mushrooms and I get to hear all about their experiences, how the shapes and the colors were moving, and the two friends who brought the mushrooms have done them before and they love this sort of thing, but for Peter and the third guy (Nick?) this was the first time and probably the last.

We hang around at the house for most of the day, play music, drink, take some other drugs, order some food, and then we go out.

It's very unfortunate that when we do go out to what is the only main bar in Palm Springs, Lloyd is also there with his friends from LA, and this is not very unusual, because everyone takes weekends to Palm Springs every now and then, but I would have hoped that someone in my group of friends who knew this might have protected me from it, but I guess they didn't know and they didn't. When I see Lloyd my heart clenches and I don't want to be there anymore and luckily Hunter and Peter understand this, so Hunter and I leave this bar (Peter stays there with his three friends) and go to the Ace Hotel, where someone heard there's a party.

The Ace party is kinda dead and there are too many straight people but at least there are some gay people we know from LA there too and these are better ones than Lloyd and his friends. In fact, the people we know from LA are Daniel, Rus, and X, and these guys are always up for some mindless good times. So Hunter and I join their group and we all exchange drugs and then one things leads to another and one hour later Daniel, Rus, X, Hunter, a random new guy that Rus found on Grindr, and I are hanging out naked in the hot tub back at the house where we're staying and everyone is high off their faces and starts fucking, and this is fine, because previously I thought that Daniel and Rus and X didn't like me for some reason, so, politically and socially, this small orgy is definitely a good idea and we will all come out on the other side liking each other a lot better. The addition of the sixth person is also genius, because he operates as a great buffer, for example, when you turn around and there's somebody there that you already know and have some history with and you don't feel like putting your dick inside right now, you grab the stranger, put him in the middle, and the awkwardness is averted. Then everyone cums and passes out and I don't know where everyone sleeps or what happens when Peter comes back to the house with his three friends after their night out, because after all the sex is over around 4:00 A.M., I decide that I'm done and I drive back to LA by myself.

SWIPE RIGHT

"I'm a very well-traveled, muscular, passionate, clever guy. Love personal one-on-one competition. Love most sports. I am not a communist, a socialist, a liberal, a snowflake, or a gay-centric person. I am a real American male that strives to be the best at whatever I am doing and I never blame others for my downfalls and travails. I am not a victim. Are you a victim? I am not 420 friendly. I love and respect my straight male friends and you should too. I am probably a lot stronger than you and I'm down to prove it. I find arm-wrestling a hot, built dude to be more thrilling than fucking or sucking. Trading gut punches in a concrete backyard with a guy makes me hard. When I drive I like to grip the top of my steering wheel high and tight so my hard tricep muscle is shown off to any dude who happens to pull up alongside of me. I've noticed that many guys will respond in kind and show off as well. I'm way too busy and I travel way too much to have a 'partner.' But I want to find one someday that can compete with me, be an equal to me, and be smart enough (or dumb enough) to keep me interested. I don't have sex the first time I meet a dude. Fucking with me first time out of the gate will be the first and last time. Try being physical with me through sports, competition, and activities and ease into it, guys, if you wanna have a real chance with me. I am OK with jumping each other instantly if the chemistry is right but don't get pissed if I don't follow up after that happens. That's how I'm wired. I am a hunter, not a collector. Most of my friends are straight males—respect that. I am most comfortable with wickedly and insanely intelligent people, or the complete opposite: dummies with no education. One stimulates my brain, the other relaxes it. I don't go to gay bars. I don't have rainbow flags in my house. I don't drive a smart car or Prius. I have a pickup, and several dirt bikes. I own power tools and know how to use them. I have several fishing poles and know how to use them. I own several guns and know how to use them. If you got a problem with that stop reading now. I don't have Twitter or Instagram or Facebook or any shit like that. I can hang with construction workers, billionaire hedge fund guys, archaeologists, plumbers, astrophysicists, Avon ladies, doctors, athletes, D.C. swamp politicians, women, men, and children and can entertain them all. The successful and wealthy teach me how to live and make my life better. The poor teach me what mistakes to avoid. Both are my friends. I feel free outdoors. I can camp in a tent above 15,000 feet and completely enjoy it. I can survive on my own out in nature for months. Try me. I am aggressive and get off on guys that are also aggressive. Wanna trade punches? Integrity. Principle. Pride. This is who I am. I don't judge people. Effeminate and gay-centric guys turn me off. Submissive guys turn me off. Fat, overweight guys turn me off. Glory to God. Muscle turns me on. Lean muscle turns me on even more. How the hell are you doing this evening?"

50

On Friday morning way before it's acceptable to open up your eyes and leave your bed I wake up and call an Uber to make my way to the airport. My flight leaves at 11:30 A.M. I'm going to Canada for my friend Ryan's wedding. Ryan used to live in London and we dated, of course, for a few weeks and then we didn't date anymore. This was years ago. Then we became friends and then everyone moved to different places around the world and fell in and out of love with several different people, but during that process Ryan met somebody who was willing to stop and marry him, so now I'm going to their wedding.

At the Canadian border control the immigration person gives me a hard time, which is surprising, as she's a girl my age or younger and I expect her to just flirt with me and wave me through. She doesn't like the fact that I'm traveling on my own, she doesn't like the fact that I'm meeting friends here (how can I possibly know these people if they live there and I live in LA? she asks, like she's never been to a circuit party before), she doesn't like the fact that my job is only part-time. Then she slowly comes to terms with all those things and she lets me in.

Then I find myself on a shuttle bus being driven to the resort where the wedding is taking place, seventy-five miles east of Ottawa. This is an adventure sports resort with water rafting, kayaking, and bungee-jumping facilities because Ryan and his new husband-to-be are very masculine, so my driver is a twenty-year-old rafting instructor in a beat-up van. Unfortunately he is not as hot as that sounds. He does spend the next couple of hours talking to me about his outdoorsy lifestyle though, how he chases the summer around the world, works at different resorts, teaches people how to raft, does all sorts of other hospitality jobs for free shelter and food and quite possibly a constant supply of weed, and I must be getting really old because none of this sounds appealing to me.

When we get to the resort he takes me to the cabin where I'm staying with a number of other people that I know from circuiting around the world, some South Africans I met in London, some New Yorkers I met in Miami, some Canadians I met on Instagram, and we all get high on some terrible coke someone flew in with from Toronto and drunk on whatever leftover drinks are lying around from the welcoming party I missed because I got here at 11:00 P.M.

On Saturday morning I wake up at nine with the rest of my house and we go get breakfast, and you have to admire their courage, because they still go and take their water rafting adventure between 10:00 A.M. to 2:00 P.M. while I go back to bed, taking prescription sleeping pills that I acquired from three different people and passing out until the late afternoon.

In the evening we all get dressed up and stand around in groups and bitch about each other, but never about the grooms, who have an incredible amount of goodwill in their favor at the moment, and very rightly so. Then we watch them get married. People make some great speeches, about love, about companionship, about the progress of gay rights in the last few years, and I'd like to feel bitter and mock all those things because I'm just so cynical, but I can't, it's all pretty great and I want a wedding like that for myself pretty much immediately, thanks.

Then we find some GHB and some MDMA and also lots more drinks, and then we dance and talk and hug and then I make out with three people and one of them sucks me off in a field behind the tent where the wedding reception is taking place and he seems to be very persistent that I cum in his mouth so he makes a really good effort for what seems like a very long time but I can't finish because I'm way too high, and then we return to the tent and I take some more G and then I start collapsing and my friends from South Africa take me back to the cabin where we're staying and give me some coke to wake me up and then I wake up and I'm quite sober and the guy from the field is now also here at the cabin with a large number of the wedding guests who have moved the party from the tent to our home and the guy wants to continue with all the oral sex but I'm really tired and over it, so I suck him off and take his load in my mouth quickly to get him off my back and then I swallow some sedatives and fall asleep on a bench right outside the cabin facing a lake, while everyone else continues to party around me.

51

On the Monday after the wedding weekend instead of going back to LA, I catch a flight and travel to London, because I was already halfway there, so why not. I'm coming down and this is not a fun flight at all and I'm really depressed right now about a multitude of things, but one of them is, of course, my single-minded obsession with pretending to want to be in a relationship, and a monogamous relationship at that, and how on earth am I ever going to be able to do that, because I can't name a single long-term relationship that I know in London or LA that doesn't involve some degree of openness.

Then I start getting some messages from this guy I slept with once when he was visiting LA who currently lives in Chicago and he's quite smart, even though he's twenty-eight and still in the closet, and we have kept in touch and right now after I complain a bit about the state of relationships in the big gay scenes that I've always lived in, the conversation goes a bit like this:

Chicago guy: Perhaps it's you who can't accept the nature of homosexuality since you want what nobody
seems to be willing or able to give. Not your fault for
wanting it. It's probably the more noble good.

Me: That's a good point. Perhaps the nature of homosexuality is eternal adolescence and polygamy.

Chicago guy: Yeah, actually it really may be. It's not written anywhere that it has to follow the same pattern as
heterosexuality.

Chicago guy: Since the latter is conducive to raising
children and the former is not.

And I don't know who is more homophobic right now: me
wanting a relationship that adheres to the heterosexual ideals
that I was brought up with or the closeted Chicago guy who
presents a theory where homosexuality is never going to be a
monogamous state, but I think it really is pretty close.

Then I get to London, where I stay for a week.

On Friday afternoon in London I invite a couple of people
over for dinner to the Airbnb flat where I'm staying in Covent
Garden, two of my closest friends, and when George arrives,
naturally, he brings with him a gram of ketamine. We start
taking this and become immobilized for a bit and watch *Come
Dine with Me* repeats, then Max also arrives and joins us and
when we run out he says that he has a surprise and pulls out
some pills that his drug dealer gave him for free last time he
bought coke and he hasn't tried them before, but we should all
take them now. These pills are called Happy-5 or Erimin and
I've never heard of them before, but a quick online research
shows that they are favored by Japanese businessmen, who

originally used to take them to relax because they are generally stressed as fuck, but they are now very popular for recreational use among experienced benzo users in Malaysia, Singapore, and Indonesia, and all this sounds like a pretty good recommendation to me. Then we take the pills, leave the flat, and walk around central London for a couple of hours and generally feel pretty chill. Then I go back home and have the best night's sleep in recent memory.

On Saturday night, I go to my friend William's, who's having a preparty before going out clubbing. There are maybe eight to ten people there. We take all the drugs and head out. We stay in the club for five or six hours, during which I make out with more people than I can count right now and have a quasi-memorable nonpenetrative threesome in the dark room with a twenty-four-year-old English guy from up north, who just came out and moved to London less than six months ago and is currently doing his first gay pride/circuit party summer parade, and an American guy my age who lives in London and is spending the entire night standing in the bathroom with his pants pulled down to his knees, lathering up his dick with water and soap from the sinks with a look on his face indicating he is so high that there is no way he will have any recollection of this the next day and taking breaks to walk into the dark room and have group sex with people he has picked up that way.

London is going through a wild drugs and sex phase right now, culturally, so much so that a new compound word has been invented to launch a million thinkpieces about gay culture: chemsex. Of course London was going through a wild drugs and sex phase even when I was living there ten years ago, but a lot more people are talking about it now, so it must be getting worse? I don't know. Maybe it is, or maybe the mainstream media finally caught up and started writing about it and now it's a self-perpetuating circle. In any case, the dating options that one has between the cities of London and LA are two. Either you choose LA and try to find someone to date in a pool of countless attractive uncultured morons with no job, or you choose London and try to find someone to date who may have a good education and a great job but prefers to spend every weekend hopping around clubs, "chill-outs" (orgies), after clubs, after-after clubs for sixty hours starting Friday evening, until he gets spat out sleepless, debilitated, and filled with regret at his desk in Canary Wharf on Monday morning just in time to miss his first meeting. There might be normal people in both cities that don't fall within either category, but those people are not in the scene, and quite frankly I don't know how to exist outside the scene (but will happily blame everyone else for it).

On Sunday evening I fly back to LA, feeling spat out.

AUGUST

52

On Saturday afternoon, I meet up with Jeremy to go to a pool party. Jeremy is somebody I met on Grindr a couple of months ago. We hooked up, kept in touch, and have had sex a couple more times since. Weeks after we first met, he started seeing somebody. He never told me this directly, but I found out from other people, because there are only about two hundred people in the gym-going gay scene of any big city and we all know each other's business. So despite not telling me, I knew that Jeremy had a boyfriend the last two times we hooked up, but I went ahead and did it anyway, because the guy that Jeremy is currently going out with made out with somebody I was dating at the time at a party a few years ago, plus he was sending Lloyd naked pictures on Facebook when Lloyd was still going out with me and living at my place. So I don't feel like I have any reason to be respectful of him and his relationship.

Jeremy and I get to the pool party where 150 of our closest friends are and act vaguely like we're dating, even though everyone knows that Jeremy has a boyfriend and, more importantly, is friends with his boyfriend. I'm guessing that the boyfriend recently did something to piss off Jeremy and I am Jeremy's way to take revenge, and that's fine by me. A few people come say hi to us and ask Jeremy where the boyfriend is, conversations that I pretend not to hear, because I am still pretending to Jeremy that I don't know he has a boyfriend, even though he knows that I know.

Then we leave and while I'm driving Jeremy home, he gets a phone call from his boyfriend. I only hear Jeremy's side of the conversation:

"Driving around."

"We're going to get some food."

"I'm with a friend."

"Konrad."

"Konrad Platt."

And then the boyfriend hangs up. I imagine this is exactly what Jeremy wanted and he must be very pleased with himself right now. I get to his house, go inside with him, we take a shower together, fuck, and I leave. Outside, I find a parking ticket on my car. I text Jeremy with, "Goddamnit, I got a ticket," Jeremy offers to pay for it because it's his street and he should have known where I'm not allowed to park, I say no, he doesn't have to do that, and I go home.

53

On Wednesday evening I'm leaving my flat to go to the gym and I'm at the stage where I'm holding my bike, I've put my headphones in, started my music, and pressed the button for the lift. This is a daring move on my part, because I don't want to be rude and usually wait to start the music until after I've exited the main entrance of the building downstairs, just in case I come across a neighbor inside the building and they happen to say hello or make any other conversation and I miss it because I'm listening to some song. Of course the one time when I have taken my chances and started playing my music immediately upon exiting my flat, Elvira opens her door, shouts my name, and comes out. I don't know if there's a facial expression when your heart sinks, but if there is, I'm wearing it right now. I stop the music and courteously pull one head-phone out.

Elvira is holding a joint but she quickly puts it out using her finger, which is highly alarming, so I can't imagine that my mildly annoyed glare will have any greater effect. As is our

usual dynamic, I am prepared to not say anything and just listen. I did contribute to the conversation one time and that one
time I told her that I was born in Germany and this seemed
highly exotic to her and she started asking me several questions about Germany, and when I pointed out I haven't lived in
Germany in twenty years and to be honest I don't even know
what goes on there anymore she wasn't deterred and now
she brings up Germany at least 90 percent of the time that she
sees me.

"I wanted to ask you, what do the Germans think of the
Greek election?" she asks, grinning like a loon.

I look over at the lift door automatically closing behind me,
shutting away my only escape route, breathe out a heavy sigh,
and say, "What election?"

The neighbor goes on to explain that there was a recent
election for president or prime minister in Greece, "whatever
they have over there," and the party that got elected will stick
it to Europe and particularly Germany (they'll say "fuck you"
to Germany, she says) and will fight for their independence
and they're badass motherfuckers and won't put up with all the
debt shit anymore. Haven't I heard?

I shake my head to indicate that I haven't.

She continues for a bit and tells me how proud she is of the
Greeks for voting for independence and then she performs a
little Greek dance to demonstrate her solidarity, an act that
involves her raising her arms to the sides and clicking her fingers while doing a few steps of something that approximates
what she might have seen in a movie, right there in our building corridor.

At that point, as an instinctive reaction, I drop my bike

sideways on the floor. This may have been involuntary, but it serves as a survival technique, because it interrupts her delirium and gives me an out. She swiftly moves on from performing the dance of Zorba the Greek to leaning over my bike and mock-stroking its handles, whispering "poor bike, you're not hurt, are you?" as I maniacally press the button for the lift again, which comes just in time when I've picked up the bike and I'm ready to go.

As the lift door closes once again with me inside this time, I hear her shout in perfect clarity: "Of course you don't know anything about the Greek election, you American, you," her tone dripping in mockery.

I ride four miles to the gym, work out my chest and biceps, first next to a very hot homophobic bro who moves away after one set when I approach him to work in with him, then next to a very hot bi-curious bro who approaches me to work in with me as soon as the first bro leaves, and ride four miles back home, listening to my iPod on shuffle, which brings up the following sequence of songs: "Hypnotease" by TEPR, "We Fly High" by Elite Gymnastics, "Mistaken for Strangers" by The National, a live version of "Declare Independence" by Björk, "Denis" by Blondie, and "Seeing Other People" by Belle and Sebastian.

54

On Wednesday evening after the gym I'm sitting at my desk doing some more work, which primarily consists of trying to learn all the lyrics to all the songs that an English punk band called Slaves has released, when I hear a knock on my door.

I open it expecting to see Elvira, but this time it's not my next-door neighbor, it's her next-door neighbor from the other side. This neighbor is another middle-aged lady who has been abusing the rent control system for the last quarter century. Her name is Linda.

Linda hands me a cell phone and tells me that Elvira wants to talk to me. On the phone, Elvira tells me that she's away for a few weeks and that while she's been away, somebody's tried to break into her apartment by taking a window screen down and opening the blinds. That's as far as they went. Now, there are always many questions when Elvira is involved and there aren't ever any answers, so I don't even bother asking them this time. The questions that form in my head and quickly disappear on this occasion are: (a) why would anyone want to break in and steal a bunch of half-burned sage, a pile of old newspapers from 1978, and twenty-five years' worth of dust (I've been in-side the apartment, I know what's in there), (b) why would anyone pull the screen and open the blinds then give up their pathetic attempt at a burglary, it's not like I or any other neigh-bor would care enough to stop them, and finally, (c) what do I have to do with this?

Before this conversation goes any further Linda tells me that she wants her phone back and can I give Elvira my num-ber so she can call me directly? And just like that, Linda is out, that crafty bitch, and Elvira has my number and my life is over.

Then Elvira calls me directly and tells me about her bur-glary nightmare and I'm convinced that despite being away she's actually orchestrated this just to create some building drama because she's bored and high somewhere faraway and she feels like she's losing her tight grip on her territory, the only place that she feels like she fully controls, our apartment building. In any case, my role in this, I find out, is to go over, wearing some gloves in order to protect any fingerprints, and pull the screen back up and close the blinds. I don't know in which order.

I say yes, that I'll go over and do that. I come out of my apartment and walk to the crime scene and Linda is standing there, hunchbacked, joyless, and mousy, and tells me that per-haps I shouldn't touch anything, gloves or no gloves, but I should tell Elvira to call the police first. Then I go back to my apartment and call Elvira to make this suggestion to her. El-vira freaks out and says that this sounds like a Linda idea, is it a Linda idea? Linda is such a meddler. I admit that, yes, this was a Linda idea. Elvira then goes on to say that she doesn't want police anywhere near her apartment, not for any reason, she doesn't want anyone in her apartment as a matter of fact, well OK, the police in particular, because of certain things she's got in there. She lets out a brief conspiratorial chuckle when she says this, and I'm not sure what I'm conspiring to, because this can range from anything like bagfuls of weed (a certainty) to decomposing, badly maintained bodies (a very strong possibility).

So anyway, the police are out, we can never call them, but I do have to go over again and close the blinds and also put tape all over the window. I don't have any tape, I say. She says, fine, do it later, can you put a note up on the door for the time being though, and I say, sure I can do that, what do you want the note to say? She says to me, are you writing this down, I can spell out any words if you don't know how to spell them because you're foreign, and I know what you foreigners are like. This is from a woman that really needs my help right now. I say no, I think I'll be fine, and she dictates: "This unit is under surveillance." At the end of that she starts spelling out "surveillance" to me anyway: "*s . . . u . . . r . . . v . . . e . . . y . . .*" Then she tells me some more about burglars in general, because we've now all signed up to this ridiculous conceit that apparently "burglars" did this, and then she gets off the phone.

I write her loony phrase on the back of a white envelope, which is the only piece of blank paper I have at home, and come out of my apartment again, where I see Linda standing there with some tape in one hand and her phone in the other. Linda tells me that here's the tape I'll need to stick the note on the door, she knows I don't have any (Elvira called her immediately after we stopped talking and let her know of my failings) and I can also use it to tape over the window if I want.

I take the tape, stick the envelope on the door, leave the tape on Linda's doorstep, and go back to my apartment. I have three missed calls from Elvira and a voice mail. I delete the voice mail without listening to it and go fill my bathtub.

55

On Friday I'm casually texting Hunter regarding my plans for the day.

Me: I just ate more than I could handle, because gains. Heading to the gym. Pray for me that at least two of my straight crushes are there, please.

Hunter: Praying. Though wait a second. You didn't go yesterday, did you? Do you really want to see them after having missed a day?

Me: Now I'm panicking.

Hunter: I'm kidding. I hope that they're there and they ask you for tips.

Me: I hope that they're there and they give me the straight acceptance my father never did.

Hunter: I hope that for you as well.

Me: Ty.

I go to the gym and do a half-arsed workout of shoulders and calves, and yes, this is a unique training combination I have just invented, and then I drive to the store, and then I drive home. I drove to the gym instead of riding my bike there because today it's raining. At least this provides some novelty in our otherwise dire existences. It also provides the opportunity for the usual five or six people to post on Facebook about how much they like the rain, the storm, the rain clouds, the wet streets, the gray skies, etc. They like it all. Because they're deep, you see? They operate on a higher level than the rest of us, who just like it to be sunny every day. Of course these people who write these posts . . . every . . . time . . . it rains . . . have never lived anywhere else other than Southern California and wouldn't move anywhere else either. I personally want to invite them to move to London for one season, say, one spring, and see what their views on the rain as a meteorological phenomenon and its effects on one's disposition will be then. Just one season.

Back at home I cook something to eat while listening to a Björk remix from 1993 that is making me really, really happy, when I receive a text from Peter. Peter is also home alone, because we all are. We all are alone. Unless you're too busy chilling or getting drunk with your roommates still, and you'll find out what a loser you are in your midthirties, possibly early forties, when life has passed you by and you end up alone. But not Peter or I. Peter and I know what losers we are now, and we are already alone.

Peter recently went on a few dates with a young idiot on steroids who's actually quite attractive and could be used as a trophy boyfriend, if that's what you're after, but you know he has nothing to give back to you. Plus he's in his late twenties and only moved to LA in the past year, so there's no hope of him having a relationship with somebody. Despite all this and despite them having nothing in common, because this younger guy, Josh, has the exact personality and depth of the back cover on the last book Peter read (paperback), I suppose Peter is also chasing them trophy boyfriends, or perhaps he's exclusively thinking with his dick and nothing else, and who can blame him, Peter thought that they could be boyfriends. So Peter took Josh out on several dates, cooked for him, tried to connect, and they did for a while, then the guy got bored and he started flaking. And he doesn't initiate plans, he cancels dates, he's slowly disappearing.

Now Peter is complaining.

"I'm going to do all the G you've left at my house tonight and kill myself."

I text back:

"Oh? Why, what's happening?"

"I tried to use it to lure Josh over tonight. But WeHo twunks were more appealing, I guess."

"What's the latest with that?"

"He's being all sweet, but he isn't really trying to close the deal. I'm being aloof but responsive."

"All right. So let me ask. Outside the physical attraction, do you have a connection with this person? Do you have common interests, things to talk about?"

"Ish. We have shared experiences. What's ur point?"

"Why all this effort?"

"There isn't much effort."

Then Peter continues:

"I wasn't even that attracted to Josh."

Yeah right.

"And, I'm not very upset about it. I've slept like a rock all week. I'm more lamenting the general lack of people to date."

"There is a definite lack of people to date."

Then Peter takes a picture of the dinner he's cooked, a dinner that would feed two people, if Josh had turned up, sends it to me, and says:

"I am eating for 2."

"We need to find you a boyfriend."

"Hope he likes fat guys."

Now, earlier in the day I took a picture of myself lying flat on my dinner table with my face against it and posted it on Instagram with the comment "high drama." So I say to Peter:

"Why don't you outpour on Instagram with a dramatic headshot against a wooden surface?"

"Been done."

"You need to find your own USP, I guess. Who are you? Why should someone date you? Find it. Post it. They will come flocking in."

"What is a USP?"

"Unique selling point."

"I'm kind, handsome, and smart. That's what I've been selling for years. I guess I need to work on the unique part."

"Yeah you need something else, sorry."

Then I explain to Peter that he needs to decide who the person that he is is, and drive it home, via social media. What's my USP? I ask him. I'm tragic and beautiful. I'm like those dumb, worked-out people, but I'm just so smart and tortured, you know? Instant USP. What's Lloyd's USP? He's a genuine, down-to-earth guy with strict morals, who loves sports, country, and family but happens to be gay. That's his

USP right there. Now, of course, our intended USP might be interpreted differently from how we want it by the wider audience, but it still counts. So instead of highly intelligent self-aware gym guy, the majority of people might look at me and think "self-absorbed queen who thinks he's smarter than he is." For Lloyd, the majority might sum it up briefly as "self-loathing dumb jock." That's fine. These are just semantics. The recipients of the message will still get it, and will still want to fuck you.

Peter gets it, but he's being lazy, so he asks:

"Why don't you think up my USP?"

I take a few seconds, restart my beloved Björk remix for what must be the fifteenth time in a row, consider that Peter has a beard, is over thirty, and makes a decent salary, and reply:

"Young daddi."

"So, more pics of me with babies?"

"It's more to do with having a grown-up lifestyle. I can see your brand coming to its own at a wine-tasting weekend, or a cooking class. I'm not saying go to these things. I'm saying that's what you could sell."

"On Tuesday night I shelled peas for the first time and made a pozole."

"There you go. Don't tell me I don't know people."

Then Peter texts me that we can work on it, that his Instagram is going to be all knees with ice packs and homemade pozoles, I text back, "sexi," and go to bed.

THREE DATES

On Wednesday morning I wake up around ten and stay in bed for another hour or so, during which I exchange naked pictures with four different people living in Hawaii, D.C., Houston, and Chicago. I forward the highlights of these exchanges to Peter and Hunter: just a series of mainly faceless body shots taken by muscular gay men in bathrooms, gym locker rooms, and bedrooms for private, yet national, distribution to other gay men they have never met.

When Peter asks me exactly how many guys I am talking to every day, I admit that I don't really know and offer to count and come up with a definitive number based on my text messages over the last three days. The rule is that if I have exchanged any flirtatious message, any shirtless or naked picture, or if I have any intention of ever sleeping with this person (or have slept with him before), they count as a romantic prospect. I go through my texts and it turns out that my current number, the number of guys I am talking to, is twenty-seven. Peter comments that this sounds like a full-time job, and maybe it is, but what else do I have to do?

Following the nationwide picture exchange, my day starts off casually with a coffee date at 3:00 P.M. This is with a gentleman I matched with on Tinder. His name is Carter. Because neither of us actually likes coffee, this ends up being a walk-on-the-beach date. Carter's strengths are his blond, flowing locks, his superhero jawline, a seemingly ideal balance between bro and prep, his perceived height, and promises of a wholesome lifestyle, full of sunsets and skiing trips and beers on the beach on tropical islands (based on his online profile anyway). Also he seems to be able to form engaging, full sentences very successfully, implying that sometime somewhere, he received a good education. The beach date goes well, Carter is smart and interesting, but he is also eleven years younger than I am, and the couple of times that our arms brush against each other as we walk on the beach my heart does not skip a beat, so I doubt we'll ever see each other again.

At 7:00 P.M., I have a second first date for the day with someone from Grindr. This is going to be a gym date. This is a gentleman called Tim, who just moved to LA from Alaska. Tim's strengths are that he's a ginger and has some very well formed pecs with really pink nipples. End of list.

Tim rocks up at my gym and within the first twenty seconds of meeting each other he's brought up dinner and asked me if I have plans and I'm not a quick enough liar to say that I do, so I guess we're now having dinner together as well. Tim is extremely talkative and loud and he's annoying the hell out of me during the workout, with a choice of such diverse topics as physical fitness ("Everyone asks me what I did to look the way that I do but I don't know, man, it just happened"), career choices and progression (he is currently studying to get a real estate license and working for a moving company where he's helping a lot of "A-list celebs like Chelsea Kane from *Baby Daddy*" move houses while creating unbreakable bonds with them, meaning that they will use him to find their next multimillion-dollar property when he's a qualified Realtor), and international politics (something about Japan and turn-of-the-century Argentina, I don't know).

Worst of all he's the first person I've ever trained with in my gym, so all the straight bros that I see every day and obsess about will now think that he's my friend and, consequently, this is what all my friends are like. I would have preferred to stay known as the mysterious, quiet fag that looks at them thirstily from a distance, with no more information as to who I might be.

After we finish this mentally excruciating workout, Tim asks how we're going to do this, are we driving in one car, are we driving in two cars, are we going straight to the restaurant, what the hell is going on, and I suggest that we stop by at my house first, get changed there, and head to the restaurant together. I'm sorry, but I might as well get something out of this, plus his thighs looked pretty good when we were doing leg presses. So we drive to my place and shower together and cum in each other's mouths and that's not something I usually go for, but I'm in my midthirties and quickly running out of all options, so I might as well get off my high horse and deal with some guy blowing his load while I'm sucking his dick and forget about it and move on.

Our shared experiences so far must be enough to convince Tim that we are now boyfriends, so on the way to the restaurant he starts referring to us as "us" and making plans for every day of the rest of the week. At one point, while we're looking for parking, he says that he'll bring his bike over and leave it at my place so we can ride around if I don't want to drive everywhere all the time.

Around 10:30 P.M. I say that I really need to get going because I have to go to bed and get up early in the morning for work.

"All right, let's go and get you to bed then," he says.

We pay and walk away from the restaurant with him holding my hand. In the lift on the way up to my apartment, where I'm hoping that he's just going to pick up his bag and leave without wanting to make out again, he says:

"It's good that you have to get up early, 'cause that means I can beat traffic."

I suddenly realize that he thinks he's going to spend the night. I tell him that I'm sorry, but I don't think this is a very good idea because I really want to take things slowly, and he eventually leaves, five full hours after we met.

Today has been really exhausting.

Just before midnight I receive a text from someone I spoke to on Grindr months ago and who lives just a few blocks away from me, but we've never met. I don't know what his name is because I never saved it on my phone. He says:

"Thinkin bout u."

I write back:

"Aw."

The rest of the conversation goes like this.

Anonymous neighbor: Whatcha up to?
Me: Getting ready for bed. You?

Anon: Just lying in bed right now. Wish I were tucking
     you in.
Me: You'll have to do that one of these upcoming nights.
Anon: I'd like to. Getting pretty impatient lol.
Me: It's coming.
Anon: What are we waiting for.
Me: An evening when we're both free.
Anon: What are you wearing?

I take a picture showing my underwear and thighs and
send it to him as a response.

Anon: Ur killin me.
Me: You like that?
Anon: Yes.
Me: Good.
Anon: I'd like it more with the boxers off.
Me: You wanna see that?
Anon: Yes.
Me: Are you sure?
Anon: Yes.
Anon: I'm sure.

I send him a stock picture of my dick.

Anon: Fuck.
Anon: That's hot.
Me: Thanks.
Anon: I'd love to see that in person right now.
Me: Show me something.

Anon: What do u wanna see?
Me: Ass.

He sends me a picture of himself lying on his front with his ass sticking up. He looks good.

Me: Damn boy.
Anon: Yeah?
Me: Aha.
Me: I wanna see that in person right now.
Anon: I'd like to show you.
Me: Why don't you.
Anon: I will. Are you inviting me over?
Me: Ye.
Anon: What's your address?

He comes over and I fuck him. He leaves, but now I can't sleep. I go on Instagram and see that Hunter is also still awake, because he's just liked a bunch of pictures. I text him:

"I had three dates today. I shook hands with the first one. Exchanged BJs with the second. And effed the third."

Hunter writes back:

"What a 'great' life."

"I know. I'm so proud that my only connections are with people I'll sleep with once and never see again."

Then I take some G and pass out.

56

Yesterday afternoon I flew to San Francisco. I'm here visiting with Willa and staying at her house, but also since I'm in a new city, I might as well find some random hookups. San Francisco counts as a new city even though I spent three months here last year, because I'm sure all the people I fucked over and the people who fucked me over, have all forgotten about each other and whatever petty grievances we had, and we are now ready to forgive each other and get drunk or high together and fuck. I have Grindr to rely on as always, of course, but I also already have a first candidate, and the first candidate is a guy called Cameron who randomly added me on Facebook about three months ago.

Cameron is possibly attractive in real life and seemed to have a nice body, but his profile didn't give too much away, there weren't enough pictures, and at the end of the day I wasn't quite sure what he looked like. Then at some point he uploaded one of those videos that people got involved with en masse for three weeks where they took off their clothes and got soaked in ice water to raise awareness for some charity and also their tight bodies, and I was sold. That video fad was very useful, in fact. Because now you could see what people's bodies looked like on video, outside a carefully posed and edited picture, plus you could hear their voices and see if they're masc (or at least if they can fake masc for three sentences, which is fine by me) or if they're just an effeminate gay with a worked-out body. So Cameron's ice bucket challenge video was quite good, he wore a robe (which, fine, was a bit fem, but passable), took off the robe, said his lines in a deep, steady voice, had the ice water thrown at him, showed us all how nice his body looks when it's wet, and I suddenly started talking to him and returning his messages. Before that he was all like "what's up, dude," "do you have Skype," "are you around tonight" and all that, and I would never respond because I don't like to jerk off on Skype because it's stupid.

So then I talked to him for a while on Facebook and then we exchanged numbers and started texting, and during those texts we would also send some naked pictures or whatever but then by the end of each exchange he would kinda freak out a little bit and ask me to respect his privacy and delete the conversations because he's not out or something, and he would promise that he also deletes the conversations from his side (like I give a shit who sees my sex talk or a picture of my dick) and I would sometimes be cordial and say, don't worry, dude, I'll delete everything, I've got your back, and sometimes I would be dismissive and tell him to stop being such a paranoid closet case and people have better things to do with their time than out some little muscle guy in the outskirts of San Francisco.

As this kept happening and as his infrequent bouts of contact and requests to Skype were often punctuated by mentions of "his roommate being away" and "having the house to himself this weekend," I started getting suspicious, or rather I didn't get suspicious, it suddenly clicked to me. This guy is not a closet case who wants to jerk off on Skype when his straight roommate is away. This guy has a boyfriend that he lives with. It just didn't make sense otherwise. People need to work on better stories. Like, how does a straight roommate stop him from showing his ass on camera to some guy in another city? Why did he have to wait for the straight roommate to be out of town in order to do that? What was he planning to do if we Skyped anyway, get naked, grab his dick with one hand, hold the laptop with the other, and tour the house?

So once I figured that out, the next time he randomly messaged me, which was a couple of weeks ago, the following conversation happened:

Closeted SF guy: What's good brotha!?

Me: All good

Closeted SF guy: Nice. I'm heading to Hotlanta today

Me: What's happening there? I'm in SF 10-12 October

Closeted SF guy: Going for work but hope to have a little fun too. Great news about coming up for an SF visit! Any plans/know where you are staying?

Me: Staying with friends and have some plans with them already, but not the whole time. Wanna eff?

Closeted SF guy: I'd love to meet ya. Too bad you will not have your own space for a little privacy

Me: Oh yeah. That's going to be a problem, I guess. Is
       your roommate your boyfriend?
SF guy cheating on his boyfriend: Yep!
Me: I'm good, aren't I?
SF guy cheating on his boyfriend: Very

Anyway, after that he took it to text messaging, because I
guess maybe he was worried the boyfriend would get access to
his Facebook messages on some home computer or something,
and he suggested that we meet up in a hotel room to "have fun"
and even though I was still not that interested in the guy, this
was now becoming a very complicated, highly dramatic, and
sleazy affair with emotional stakes and general ridiculousness, so
I suddenly got really into it and said, "Yes, let's go to the hotel,
let's be really dirty and sordid and immoral," and I asked him
to book it and he did, and this got even better because it turned
from a hotel to a really cheap, disreputable motel in the center
of the city where people just go to fuck, even though one of the
people is a hooker most of the time, you know, the kind of
motel that has bright fluorescent lights everywhere, and a soda
machine in the parking lot, and a balcony that surrounds the
parking lot where the doors to all the rooms are, like you see in
some indie movies. And the whole sordid affair really turned
me on, and this is how I found myself getting out of an Uber
and buying a can of Coke from a soda machine in the parking
lot of a cheap motel and waiting for my Facebook date to come
back from the convenience store where he's gone to buy a
bottle of whiskey or whatever it is he's buying in order to mute
his conscience and manage to get through this.

I cross the street and walk up to the convenience store where he is. I see him at the till and I wait outside, because I don't want the guy who works there to see us saying "nice to meet you" and hug for the first time, and realize that we don't know each other but we're about to go fuck in that motel across the street. This is all in my head, of course, and the guy who works there doesn't give a shit, or even if he is bored enough and likes to make up stories about his customers, it doesn't necessarily follow that he would think these two gay guys just met, one of them is already drunk and just bought another bottle of vodka, they are definitely going to the motel across the street to fuck. Wait, now that I've heard it in my head, this is exactly what he would think. There is absolutely no other interpretation of what's happening here from the convenience store employee's vantage point. The question is, should I care?

My Facebook date comes out and we hug uneasily. He is definitely drunk and also shorter than I thought. His body is good, lean and tight in a way that photographs well, though I prefer bulkier frames, and I probably should start drinking as well. We walk back to the motel, crossing the street on a red light because we don't have much to talk about, so we want to hurry up to avoid the awkwardness, and go up the external staircase that leads to the outside balcony where the door to our room is. Once inside, I pour myself a drink from the bottle he's just bought. He's also bought ice, as well as plastic cups, because he didn't feel the glasses provided by the motel were clean enough. He was right. I excuse myself pretty much immediately and take my drink to the bathroom. I check myself in the mirror, undo my trousers, take down my underwear, and quickly rinse off my dick in the sink, because, I don't know, I always do that when I know it's about to get sucked or whatever. I pat it dry with one of the face towels provided and do my trousers back up. I notice that he hasn't used any of the towels himself, nor the soap provided, which remains packed in its cheap little piece of motel paper by the sink. Perhaps if he didn't want to touch the glasses, he didn't want to touch anything in the room, I don't know.

I come outside and stand on the opposite side of the bed to him. He's fiddling with a drink by an area he has customized as a little bar, and asks me if I want another. I do. I walk over to him to have my cup refilled and ask whether he's tried putting the TV on. He seems surprised and says no. I say maybe there's a music channel we can put on or something. I find the remote and turn it on and flick through channels, although I don't find one that's playing music videos nonstop because this is not 1997, and he suggests that he play something using Spotify on his phone. I say, sure. He puts on some DJ podcast or something and asks me if I like it, and I say yes because there is no chance he would ever have randomly chosen something I actually like, so I decide to leave it. The music is very quiet and tinny anyway. We start making out and take each other's clothes off. My initial assessment of his appeal remains. He is sexy enough but not exactly my type. Which is clearly for the best. As he has a boyfriend. And arranges anonymous hookups behind his back. In sleazy motels. And I'm not sure I want to be really into someone like that.

We continue making out and I know already that I don't really want to fuck, but I guess I'm here now, so I go along with it for a while. We are now both naked in bed. After a while he starts sucking me off and he does it so persistently that I'm going to cum. "I'm going to cum if you keep doing that," I say. He stops sucking me off and I ask if he wants to fuck. He's says that he's down to fuck, but then we remember that neither of us has brought condoms or lube. He says, all right, we can cum now, then take a break, go buy some condoms and lube, come back, and fuck. We have all night here, after all. I don't like the sound of any of this, so I say yes. He goes back to sucking me off until I cum. Now I'm completely over it. He says that that was very hot and he can't wait to fuck later. I agree that it will be totally hot and help him jerk off in the meantime. Once he also comes, he says, you know what, I don't think I need to fuck, this was so hot by itself. I thank whatever God exists, lie in bed with him reflecting back on what an incredible hookup we just had for approximately twenty seconds, then I book an Uber to go back home and start getting dressed. By the time I've found all my clothes, the Uber is here, we say good-bye and, once again, that this was totally hot, and I leave.

57

On Friday I am expecting the arrival of Jake Burke, who is a tall, blue-eyed, muscular Denver, Colorado, resident in possession of a smartphone and a Facebook account, which means that we have spoken online for weeks and that he is now flying over to LA to stay at my place for the weekend. All the preliminary signs that this is going to be awful are there. First of all, Jake Burke is a DJ at a gay bar. Second of all, he exclusively wears high-tops. Third of all (although just the first two would be more than enough), a few days ago I had the following conversation with a friend of mine who lives in Denver and knows Jake.

Me: Hello. Do you know "Jake Burke"?
Denver friend: I do.
Me: Is he nice?
Denver friend: He isn't coming to stay with you. Is he?
Me: Yes [frown emoticon]. Is this TERRIBLE?
Denver friend: Ummmmmm. He is nice. He is attractive.

We have been friends for yrs. He has nothing to
say.

Me: I like him already.

Denver friend: And he isn't the brightest.

Me: I see.

Denver friend: I have no idea what you will talk about.

Me: I'll take him to do activities, show him shiny stuff?

Denver friend: I do like Jake. But I'm trying to imagine
your weekend together and I just can't.

I pick up Jake at the airport and it's 9:00 P.M. and he's all
set and ready to go out to the bars, but I suggest that perhaps,
since we've never seen each other in real life before, we could
probably stay in, have some dinner, say some words to each
other, fuck. The disappointment is palpable and it takes a lot
of reassurance that yes, we can still get really drunk and high
even if we stay in, and then we stay in and get drunk and high,
but there is no fucking, because by the end of all the drugs
nobody can get it up and I've run out of Cialis.

On Saturday morning, I wake up before ten thirty and find
Jake in the kitchen, already mixing up powders from the carry-
on bag that he's brought with him (in addition to his small suit-
case of high-tops and clothes), which contains exclusively gym
supplements. This is something that he's pointed out to me
several times since he arrived, the fact that he needs to check
extra luggage for supplements when he travels, so I take it he
must be quite proud of it. I'm kinda sleepy and want to chill
the eff out, but he's pumped up from whatever combination of
cracky preworkouts he has taken and wants us to go to the
gym. I ask whether he actually wants to waste part of his LA

weekend lifting weights when there's five hundred other things we could be doing, but he informs me that it's only four months until Sydney Mardi Gras, where he's going, and he's really sorry but he's not going to compromise his training schedule now, cutting it so close. (He does not actually say "compromise." I am upwardly paraphrasing.) He then shows me an actual countdown of workouts until Sydney Mardi Gras that he has created and keeps on his phone. It's very elaborate and must have taken hours to put together, but at least it provides some insight as to what he does with his downtime between Sundays and Fridays when he's not using his laptop to stream Ariana Grande remixes for the dancing gay crowds of Denver.

We go to the gym and work out separately, partly because we've already started not being able to stand each other, and partly because I don't actually want to work out, as I'm getting a weird kickback reaction to his apparent gym obsession. I expect that if I spent any significant time with this person, I would probably just quit the gym altogether. And if I weren't a gym-obsessed, judgmental, insecure gay cliché, who would I be?

On the way home we stop at the grocery store to buy some food and he also buys three bottles of wine. He has finished the first bottle of wine in the time it takes us to go back home, shower, and get ready for the beach. It's always fun for everyone around when people choose to get drunk alone. We walk down to the beach, where at least I get the opportunity to use Jake to enhance my social media profile by posting a picture of him looking stacked and adding the tagline "some boys are bigger than others," paraphrasing the Smiths' song, because now everyone will see that I'm hanging out with someone who's bigger than all my exes, and that's extremely important for some reason. People will also assume that we're sleeping together, I'm guessing, and the truth of the matter doesn't actually count for anything, because truth is by default what the majority of people believe. Truth is a story. Truth is not a fact. I am sleeping with Jake.

On Saturday evening Jake gets his wish, as we get high as fuck and go out in West Hollywood. Jake chooses to supplement his GHB dosage with a steady intake of alcohol throughout the night, a practice that is very dangerous and can even be lethal, but does contribute to such a high intensity of buzz if you're lucky enough to stay alive that you might even be fooled into thinking you are having a good time in a half-empty WeHo gay bar on a mid-October Saturday night. For better or worse he does stay alive and we stay out until 3:00 A.M. when Jake decides that he's had enough and we're finally allowed to go home.

On Sunday he wakes up and goes to the gym, but this time I stay at home. When he comes back, I really want to torture him a bit, so I insist that his LA experience must also be a cultural one and we need to go to a museum. It's now 1:00 P.M., so he drinks a bottle of wine, puts on some high-tops, and we head out. I take him to the Getty Villa in Malibu. We speed-walk through the exhibits for the next twenty minutes as he does his best not to murder me, and I don't know why, but I'm really enjoying this. Once or twice he takes breaks from staring at the floor, sulking, and glances up to make useful contributions showcasing a very loose grasp of time and space in historical terms, and I don't remember exactly all the things that he says, but I do remember that at some point he

tries to argue with me that, in the past, the United States had
a monarchy. This conversation goes a little bit like this.

Jake: I wonder who used to live here in the old days.
   Probably some king or something.
Me: I don't think so. You never had a king.
Jake (very subtly unsure of himself but with the forced
   conviction of an idiot who does not want to back
   down): You don't know that.
Me: I think I do.

Then we go back home, and we avoid each other for the
next few hours, and then I drive him to the airport, hoping
never to see him again. As soon as I drop him off I text:
"Thanks so much for coming, this was a really fun weekend."
He writes back:
"No, thank you for everything. I had a really good time."
And we never speak again.

58

On Saturday afternoon I am scrolling through Facebook and some WeHo guy on malfunctioning steroids has posted a picture from a gay photo shoot he must have done and is really proud of, wearing just white Emporio Armani briefs and holding a very sultry pose. He has uploaded this with the tagline "Sexy Saturday." I take a screenshot and send it to Peter, adding: "I beg to differ." Then I go to the gym.

59

On Saturday morning I go to the gym, where I'm supposed to work out my shoulders and back, but mainly my shoulders, because they have been a weak point for a very long time and it's getting really embarrassing. I'm doing a set of new exercises that I've never done before, and this is really stressing me out, making me walk around the gym looking lost, holding an iPhone up that's playing fitness YouTube videos, trying to make sense of it all.

For my first exercise, which somebody somewhere named standing barbell military press, I need a barbell. There's one barbell on an incline bench nearby, so I walk over to it and start picking it up. Then some guy comes back and tells me that he's still using it. Then I stand there again more lost, but now also disappointed. Then I notice that my straight gym crush (one of the top twenty-five anyway) who's using a different barbell on a different incline bench right next to me is trying to make cautious eye contact and catch my attention, but in a very tentative way, plus I'm wearing headphones and he can't really talk to me.

This seems like it goes on for an eternity if the feeling in my lower abdomen is anything to go by, but in human time-and-space terms it's probably only two to three seconds before he actually opens his mouth, I remove my left headphone, and he asks me to spot him for one last set, and then I can have the barbell if that's what I'm looking for. This is exactly what I'm looking for and a little bit more, so I mumble "sure" and I go stand behind him as he's doing one last set of incline chest presses while I breathe in each time he exhales in agony in the general direction of my face.

My straight gym crush is about six three, has very short, light brown hair and an outdoor tan, the face of a G.I. Joe action figure but with hesitant eyes, and a tight, muscular, yet lean upper body. He also has really big, strong legs, perhaps more muscular than his upper body, which is pretty much my favorite thing anyone can have, and I assign this to him playing some particular, highly imaginary sport that mainly utilizes lower-body strength, even though my friend Hunter says that I'm just making this up because I want this guy to be a masc jock who kills it at sports, but it's just probably the way he's built.

For this exercise he was going for six reps, he said, but he only manages five, with my assistance needed for only the last one. We quickly recover from this highly sexual activity (in my head only, but still) by removing the weights from the barbell together.

"How many do you want on?" he asks.

"None of them," I say.

He takes one side and I take the other, and he really doesn't have to do that, so I stutter "thank you" and "thank you so much" an inordinate amount of times as he goes between the barbell and the weight rack.

Then we're done and I'm about to remove the barbell and take it away and he walks up to me one last time with a face that hasn't shown any expression throughout our interaction apart from physical strain as he was doing his exercise, offers his hand for a fist bump, which I incompetently return, and says:

"Thanks, boss."

I die a few deaths inside, and continue with my workout, both ecstatic and also devastated, in the way that you would feel if you knew you had just been touched by the hand of God . . . via a fist bump . . . while he called you "boss," but having no way to tell if the experience will ever be repeated, or if that right there was your life peaking and you're now faced with slow, excruciating drudgery until you finally expire thirty or forty years from now.

Hunter and Peter are away for the weekend, so in order to fill the rest of the day, I have arranged to go on two first dates with people I've met online. This is going to be a real stretch in terms of socializing, and at this point I have about 0 percent confidence in myself that I'm going to go through with both, but these are two people I have avoided meeting and even canceled on already over the last few months, and this month I'm trying to be less of an asshole, so we'll see.

I meet the first date at a shopping mall in Santa Monica. It's 4:30 P.M. He doesn't have a plan of what he wants us to do and neither do I, so I suggest that we go to GNC to buy some supplements, because, you know, these are the people we are and these are the things that we do. At GNC I buy a bulking protein powder that has a thousand calories per serving and you're supposed to take once a day in addition to your regular meals to put on weight, but last time I bought it I found that it was so filling that after I drank this thick, potent chocolate-flavored sludge, I felt so sick that I couldn't eat for the rest of the day, therefore completely defeating its purpose. Perhaps this time it will work better.

After GNC we walk around and have some ice cream, then we walk down to the beach and watch the sunset. I think he and I have enough conversation for just over an hour, but around 5:45 P.M. we're basically just standing there, watching the sun sinking into the ocean in complete silence. He checks his phone, I check my phone, he asks me what I'm doing later, I say that I'm meeting some friends for dinner at 8:00 P.M. and he wonders how much time is left on the meter where he parked. We decide that it's imperative that we go and check to avoid him getting a ticket, even though I distinctly remember that he said he paid for three hours when we met at 4:40 P.M., as it seemed highly ambitious to me even back then.

On the way to the car, he asks me whether I want to walk back home or if he can give me a lift, and I take the lift. When we get there and he's about to drop me off, he remembers that he needs to use the bathroom before he drives off, so I offer that he come upstairs, and he does just that. He leaves his car on the street double-parked with the hazard lights on. He comes upstairs, uses the bathroom, we tell each other what a nice time we had, move in for an awkward good-bye hug, start making out, go to the bedroom, he tells me that he has something to say to me and hopes it's all right, I say go on, he says that he's HIV positive but undetectable, I say that's fine, thanks for telling me, I'm on PrEP but I wasn't planning on having unprotected sex anyway, and then we fuck.

When this is all done, I want to go on the second date so little that I'm thinking of drowning myself in the bathtub to get out of it. I fill it up and climb in, but I can't bring myself to go through with it, so I suppose this suicide attempt will just have to serve as an actual bath, and I will just have to go on a second first date in the space of four hours.

My second first date picks me up from home at 8:30 P.M. We drive to Abbot Kinney in Venice to find a place to eat. Clearly I haven't booked anywhere, since only forty-five minutes earlier I was thinking of terminating my own life to avoid being here. My date is a very hyper, self-proclaimed type A–personality little guy on steroids, talking six thousand words a minute, living his life on a constant preworkout high.

We drive past a restaurant we both like the look of. He decides to call them from the car to see if they have any space for us. He connects through the car stereo and talks to the hassled Australian hostess. His opening line is:

"Are you on a wait right now?"

This is very confusing for me, as well as to the unfortunate girl on the other end of the line, who has to decipher his weird choice of jargon through the poor connection of a moving vehicle, plus the loud conversation of the 120 people she's standing in the middle of at a packed restaurant on a Saturday night. Once he rephrases to something more conventional/human, we are able to acquire the information that, yes, they are very busy, of course, but there are some cancellations and they will be able to fit us in. My date then proceeds to enquire whether they have a table in a "nice garden area," despite not knowing what the layout of the restaurant is like at all, although having just driven past and seen that there is no outdoor space might have cleared that up. The hostess laughs in an uncomfortable way that indicates she is now aware she's dealing with a lunatic who has no intention of eating there tonight, and says that, no, unfortunately they don't have a garden area. Not quite done yet, my date then asks if they possibly have a "booth" we can sit in, the hostess says in an icy tone that we'll have to come in and see what's available then, my date says awesome, see you in a bit, we park the car and go to a different restaurant.

I am back home alone by 11:00 P.M. eating leftovers that I brought home in a box and watching repeats of *Poirot* on Netflix.

60

On Saturday this week, Peter, Anthony, Hunter, and I decide to go down to Laguna Beach and spend the day at Hunter's parents' house. Hunter's parents are away for the weekend. This is part of an overall plan to diversify our activities and not do things that revolve exclusively around the gay bars in West Hollywood and Grindr. After fighting off conflicting ideas from Peter, who wanted us to go to San Diego or Las Vegas and spend the weekend at gay bars there and with a whole new set of Grindr search results, four of us drive down to Orange County on Saturday morning.

Orange County is a lovely, beautiful place that you have to be extremely unfortunate to have been born and brought up in, for no other reason than that, if you're from there, you really have to go out of your way to experience what the rest of the world has to offer. If all you've ever known is eternal sunshine, your parents' swimming pool, and the golf course at the local country club, why pick up a book to read reflections on human existence written by some dead guy from the last century?

Why ever move to Copenhagen for a year? If you're born there, you already are where everyone else is trying to get through their life journey, but instead of getting there at fifty-five after thirty years of hard work and having learned all your life lessons, you just land in your beautiful, formulaic mansion as an infant.

This Saturday, we celebrate Hunter's dad's achievements by spending the whole day swimming in the pool, shooting hoops in the basketball court, and hanging out in the Jacuzzi. I take it as a huge personal achievement that I don't text any sexual prospects for the whole day and don't seek romantic validation from any of the men that I otherwise talk to. If I actually believed that humans can progress, I would think this is growth.

Then it really becomes apparent that, indeed, there is no growth at all, because we all get bored and decide to go back to LA and go out. There is always the severe danger that if I step out anywhere in Los Angeles on a Saturday night Lloyd will be there and I will see him and my heart will crack in new places where it hadn't cracked before, but at this point I am too drunk and too high for this to be a concern that will stop me.

First we go to some house party up in the hills. The only thing that we know about this house is that it's owned by some exceptionally rich guy from New York who only comes to LA a couple of times a year and this is not one of them. In the absence of the house owner, the party is hosted by his young, unattractive boyfriend, and the few bits of information that this person decides to share while he's giving us a tour of most of the rooms and all of the servants, are the following: he used to be an actor, he is now still an actor but also working on a few writing projects, the house chef really excelled himself with the dinner he prepared earlier, and the only instruction that was given to the architects who redesigned the house last year when it was purchased was "there is no budget." I don't know if those people come up with these lines on the spot, or if they practice them alone first and then bring them out in group situations, or . . . I don't know. It's baffling.

Then I see a guy at the party who's relatively attractive, via having nice biceps and a very full ass anyway, and I believe I'm friends with him on Facebook though I've never met him before because he lives in New York also, so I decide to dedicate the rest of my evening to him. His name is Porter. Porter reveals early on in our interaction that he has a boyfriend back home, but he's also pushing his butt against my crotch while making out with another guy when the three of us go into one of bathrooms to share some coke, so the messages that I'm getting here are somewhat conflicting. In any case, this seems like a fun evening and I decide to follow those two out to the bars of West Hollywood when they decide to leave the party.

We walk into the first bar, in practical terms a tiny cube of a room playing annoying 1980s disco pop, and immediately bump into Lloyd. He's right by the entrance, standing there with three men that unfortunately the third person in my group happens to know. We all stand in a circle as they say their hellos and I avoid looking in the direction of Lloyd. I'm introduced to the people I don't know by the third guy, and the next time I look around Lloyd has disappeared. He hasn't just walked away, I can see pretty much everyone in this small room; he has actually left the bar. For some reason this really pisses me off. About ten minutes later, Porter and the third guy have decided that they really can't stand the music in here,

apparently, and want us to leave too. We go out, cross the
street and walk into the next bar. Lloyd is here again, this
time by himself. He sees me walk in, our eyes meet, he turns
his back to me and walks to the bar. I tell Porter that I'll be
right back. My state of mind is extremely unsettled and I'm
almost hyperventilating. My heartbeat has just about doubled.

I push my way through the dance floor crowd and grab his
arm to turn him around at the bar. He pretends that he hadn't
seen me before and says hi. For about eight seconds we make
small conversation through gritted teeth and then I decide
that this is the right time to demand answers to all the questions I've had for him, so I unleash a very angry and aggressive
tirade. I ask him why he led me on and pretended to be interested in me when he wasn't. Why he moved into my place
when he never wanted to be my boyfriend. Why he told me he
loved me. Why he never had sex with me. I ask why he lied to
me about everything when I first met him last summer. About
his job, about the people he had slept with, about wanting to
go out to the gay bars all the time. Why he would freak out
and attack people for using Grindr or exchanging naked pics,
when it turned out that he was doing the same thing. The
number of answers I get is approximately the number that exists inside his head, which equals zero. Or rather, I know the
answers, probably better than even he does; I don't know exactly why I'm doing this. Then I decide to focus for a bit on the
money that he owes me and refuses to return, which is equally
ineffective. Eventually, with no answers and no cash trans-
ferred over, we walk away from each other. He walks upstairs
to the next floor. I go back and find Porter, who's making out
with the third guy on the dance floor. I join them and start

making out with Porter as well, who's now dancing between us. Porter grabs my hand and puts it down his underwear, so I proceed to finger him as he takes turns to kiss us both.

Soon after that, we get an Uber to go back to the rich guy's house up in the hills, where my car is parked and Porter is staying for the weekend. I'm under the false impression that for the next hour or so Porter will also be taking turns in getting fucked by the two of us, but when we get to the front gate, Porter says that, despite him wanting me to, I can't come in because the rich guy's boyfriend who showed us around before didn't like me and, he's sorry, but he has a place on the rich guy's dinner party rotation and he's not about to piss him or his boyfriend off and lose it. So I get in my car and drive home by myself.

61

On Monday I wake up and see that the sun is out and it's really warm, but I'm too lazy to walk the six minutes it would take me to get to the beach, so I go up to the roof of my building and sit there on the deck to sunbathe. I do have a book with me to read, but I'm more preoccupied with texting people on my phone and checking social media.

Today I am mainly focusing on Greg Marconi, who is texting me from Orlando. We've never met, of course, but are Facebook and Snapchat friends. Greg has a minor crush on me, it seems, but I am not interested at all because he is a lawyer, has an Italian surname, and has adopted a boastful/hyperconfident flirting technique in order to impress me. Little does he know that he is doing it all wrong and that I exclusively fall for Anglo-Saxon insecure underachievers. Today Greg is telling me the following in order to make me jealous and win my long-distance affection (which, fair enough, is not the highest prize and that at least several hundred unfortunate men have enjoyed in the past year alone for a maximum of two weeks).

Greg: "I broke someone's heart last week"

This statement alone is naturally an instant eye roll, but on top of that I also find it quite unpleasant and unnecessarily cruel, because I have a chip on my shoulder about having my heart broken and I don't think people should be joking about it or showing off. So he's lost me already today. I reply:

"Standard week for Greg Marconi, I imagine"

"You know me too well."

And he continues:

"He was a Facebook celebrity and fell in love after the first time we hung out. I like him but he came on too strong"

"Name?"

"Jack Novak, in real life. Aka Jack Joseph on Facebook."

"Oh. We're friends also. He seems perfectly balanced. I have no idea why it didn't work."

"Everything was OK until he cried when I left to drive home"

"He posts videos of himself flexing, dancing, and singing to the camera ripping off his T-shirt halfway through. This is not a dateable person"

"Yeah but he was man of the day on RealJock once. That's actually how I first knew about him lol . . ."

"I take it all back"

"In other news, my ex and I have been talking some"

"Interesting. It's all happening around there, isn't it"

"Never a dull moment"

Then Greg asks me if I want to go to Pensacola for Memorial Day weekend, then I tell him that Pensacola and the rest of the South is populated by a bunch of drunk, god-fearing, gay-issue-ridden twenty-year-old idiots, and then the conversation trails off and I am getting sunburned, so I go back inside.

There, I eat something because it is now lunchtime, get ready for the gym, and text Hunter with:

"I'm getting ready for the gym"

Hunter replies immediately:

"I'm working out at a gym in Culver City because I had a work meeting here. So much sex everywhere"

"Inconspicuous straight bros, right?"

"Yes. There seems to be a subtle league of the hottest ones. They all help spot each other and exchange casual laughs. I want in"

"You may torture yourself for several months . . . but they will never let you in. Accept it and just observe"

"My youthful, nonjaded spirit refuses to believe this"

"OK then. Just go up to the group and ask them if they think that RiRi killed it at the American Music Awards red carpet this weekend like you were texting me last night and see if they welcome you into their group"

Then I don't think Hunter goes up to them and talks to them, and then I go to the gym.

When I come back I go online, because that's where I live, and read comments that members of the Popjustice forum have left about the American Music Awards attendees while I eat my postlunch.

Reacting to Beyoncé's red carpet look, member "TasteMe" has written:

"YAAAAAAAAAAAASSSSSSSSSSSSSSSSSSSSSSSAT HER BODEYYYY!!!!!!!!!!!"

And:

"MURDERRRRRRRRRRRRRRRRRRRRRr MEHH-HHHHHHHHHHHHHHHHHHHHH"

"Psychic" has replied:

"Oh. Seems try-hard"

But "TasteMe" is really feeling it and has added:

"Beysus is serving for the GODS and I'm living. That's all that matters"

On Rihanna's red carpet look, "KellyRowlandsWeave" has commented:

"Hmm. Serving me Ashanti 2002 teas"

But "ShadyMatt" really liked it (I think), because he said:

"Rih is giving me bejeweled omelet on a platter"

I read several pages of comments that go like this until the very end, where "TaylorsGrammy" has magnanimously commented, "All the Big Pop Girls brought IT," and then I go out to watch the sunset on the beach.

62

On Thursday night I'm at home reading the last of *Nausea* once again and listening to *Louder Than Bombs,* and this might as well be 1994 and I might as well be a teenager in a suburban bedroom in Berlin, but I'm not, it's twenty years later, and I'm in a house in Venice instead and I think those are the only two things that have changed.

At eleven thirty I text Hunter to say that life is very lonely and he writes back to tell me that he had nothing to do this evening and felt very alone and couldn't stay in his room another night. So he went to the park near his house, laid on the grass, and watched a softball game from afar and it was such a nice time. And of course he would like someone to join him, but he enjoyed it. And there's no moral to his story, he says, but yes.

Then I text Peter with the screenshot of a guy who friend-requested me on Facebook and ask him what he knows about this guy, if anything. Peter writes back that he's a nice guy, he met him while volunteering for some charity project in LA, he has a big butt, huge, but he's too short for me.

I write back, "Right. Maybe worth a fuck then," and I go to bed.

63

On Friday morning Elvira decides to wake me up right before eight by banging on my front door very loudly. As per usual, I'm inclined to ignore her until she tires and goes away, but I'm awake now, plus this will be my first opportunity to talk to a real-life person this week, so I get up and answer. This is a terrifying thought, but we might be becoming codependent.

She bursts into my apartment, takes a seat on the sofa, and launches into the reason why she had to talk to me so urgently. Apparently, our building is being targeted by a gang. I suppose that is a good enough reason.

She was just drinking her morning coffee while staring outside the window, when she noticed a vehicle she did not recognize parked in front of our entrance. Then she noticed its driver (a young man) behaving "oddly but not illegally." He was walking around the vehicle nervously, opening and closing windows and doors and generally pacing in an unusual manner. At one point he reached inside the passenger-side window and took something that appeared to be a piece of white chalk. He bent down and appeared to be writing something on the sidewalk. She has now checked this firsthand and there is a white chalk mark where he was crouching. After doing this, the young man got up suddenly and quickly returned to his vehicle, got into the driver's seat, turned around, and drove away. This gave her the chance to note the vehicle model and license number. Elvira then asks me to write this down. I haven't said anything so far, but now I tell her I don't have anything to write with. She says that's fine, but I should memorize it. It was a late-model white Ford Expedition with the license 8HAI550. I tell her that I got it. Then I ask when the gang is coming over.

She tells me that she's not sure exactly what happens next, but she's convinced our building was marked for a hit. These guys are becoming more and more sophisticated, she says. "Yes, they have chalk now," I tell her. She says that's right and what will probably happen is that the gang will come and rob us and then the police will compare the chalk mark with other existing marks in other break-ins and make the connection and solve all the crimes. Then she wants us to go downstairs and take a picture of the mark "to keep on file," but I'm not ready to leave the house at 8:20 A.M., I'm sorry, so I tell her that I have to go back to bed now, but I will definitely go and do that later, and she leaves and I go back to bed.

64

On Friday, I wake up at 7:00 A.M. but it's too early and I have nothing to do today anyway, so I take half a tab of Zopiclone, eat a banana and drink a protein shake because I don't know when I will wake up next and I don't want to lose any meals, and I go back to sleep. When I wake up again it's 11:30 A.M.

I check my phone and I have a couple of messages that are from people who are not significant to me right now and a missed call from my mum and I will call my mum back, I promise, but first I make a second breakfast and sit and eat while checking Facebook.

Jeff Diaz, a very attractive Latino guy who is a personal trainer and an actor or fitness model and dancer that I met at a pool party a few weeks ago, has written an update that says:

"Decided on a whim today that I'm going to focus on gaining some weight. I knew I was going to do it, just not sure when. Looks like today is the day due to the fact that I am tired of #GrilledChicken and #SteamedBroccoli and if I have to eat that as another meal, something unpretty might just go down. I now get to use the next few months changing my diet and enjoying eating the right, flavorful foods that will get me to where I want to be for the time being. Hello #WholeFat Milk #WholeFatCottageCheese #PeanutButter #Weight Gainer #QuestBars

"Today I'm at 183 lbs and the goal is 195/200 lbs then I will lean out when I am satisfied. #LeanMuscle I'm hoping it all goes to my butt #Booty #BootyBuilder

"#HollywoodLife #InstaFit #MuscleGain #QuestBars #Muscle #Lean #HollywoodBody #CaliforniaLiving #Fit ness #ChangeUp"

I screenshot this and send it to Peter.

Gabriel Franklin, an aspiring young actor I went on a date with recently, even though he has a boyfriend, something that I found out later and then declined going on a second date with him because it pissed me off that he hadn't told me, even though in reality I just wasn't that attracted to him and I used this as an excuse, has written an update that says:

"Things I want for my birthday: money, new Ray-Bans, jalapeño margaritas, socks, a pair of dope chubbies, cool Vans, a new car . . . BMW and above, abs, an even tan, dark chocolate with almonds, wine, money, 55in TV and above, no cheap shit, a brown ass watch, a trip to Hawaii, bananas, a pretzel, a recurring role on a show . . . make that lead role, tequila, croutons, a badass part with all my friends telling me they all love me. Thx."

I also screenshot this and send it to Peter and add, "You can really tell when someone's grown up dirt poor, can't you," and then I start looking for some porn to jerk off to.

As a first step, I visit a blog that's updated daily with screen-shots and reviews of every new porn scene that all the major gay porn studios release. Even though I've come across this blog before, I've never really stayed on it long enough, nor have I paid attention, but I suppose for someone as idle and lonely as I am, it was only a matter of time before going back and getting lost in the vortex that it is, and today the time has come. For the next hour or so, I go through several posts, look at endless pictures of people having sex, and read whole pages of reviews. I identify two or three favorite scenes and then find them online to download for free. I don't want to stream them and get off immediately; I want to delay this as long as possible. As I wait for the huge files to download (because nothing less than HD will do) I go back to the individual blog entries and read the dozens of comments that other socially inept porn addicts have left. This is a new community that I am today becoming a part of, and I think I really like it. People seem to have very strong views about the men that appear in these scenes. People seem to know them, and people seem to have very strong preferences about their appearance, body hair, body transformation over the course of time and between scenes, how they take the d, how they give the d, whether they are gay in real life or gay-for-pay (G4P is a new acronym in my life), whether they flip-flop in the scenes or are strict tops or bottoms, what steroids they should be on, when somebody has taken too many steroids, and how they have advanced from entry-level studios with bad lighting and minimal direction to more professional ones where they're finally reaching their potential. I'm starting to find this aspect of pornography even more sexually gratifying than watching the sex.

Then my first scene has downloaded, and I watch the entire half-hour clip until the end without touching myself at all.

When that's over, I start watching the second scene, which is now also ready. Again, I watch the whole thing but blow my load in a pair of underwear I've picked out of the laundry basket near the end when all the performers also cum.

It's now around 3:00 P.M. I go back on the blog and search by name to find more clips from my two favorite porn actors from the two clips I've just watched. I find a couple more clips that I think I will like and start downloading them. I go back and read the comments that people have left for those, and then watch the third clip that I had previously ignored. I jerk off to this and cum about halfway through.

As I wait for the latest two scenes to download, I realize that I haven't eaten anything for a few hours and take a break from staring at my computer screen to make a snack.

At 4:30 P.M., I go back and watch the two new clips back to back, ejaculating at the end of each one. I have now cum four times in the last five or six hours. The fact that I am now a sad, lonely loser who has spent the whole day jerking off is making me feel disgusted with myself but is also turning me on. I want to see how far I can take it. I go back and find more videos that I want to watch. I start downloading them, and then step away from the computer again to take a break, during which I read about five pages of *The Tunnel* by Ernesto Sabato, which is my favorite book that I've started reading this year, but I am completely distracted by porn right now, so I go back and start rewatching my recent clips.

By 8:00 P.M., I have jerked off another two times. Because I feel worthless and because I am realizing that this could easily be the beginning of a serious sociopathic condition, I force myself to get dressed and go to the gym to work out. At the gym I just picture everyone having sex anyway and get really annoyed when neither the receptionist who's relatively hot, nor this blond kid in the weights area who's actually very hot, make embarrassing small talk with me, then proceed to take their clothes off and start sucking me off before we all fuck together in the locker room, so I do a half-arsed workout for forty minutes and then go back home. I watch two of the clips again, and cum for a seventh time today.

I follow this up by watching YouTube clips of Joni Mitchell performing "Both Sides Now," first in 1970 and then in 2000, and this makes me really, really fucking sad, like, I don't know, my life is halfway over and I haven't even reached any great epiphanies yet, and then I start texting my friend Anthony to ask him how his trip back to London has been. Instead of texting me back, he FaceTimes me and I'm feeling brave so I answer and we talk for a while, then he brings up this guy that I went on a date with last week, asks me how it was and whether I want to see him again, and I think back, answer that the guy picked me up in a Fiat 500 and, really, there's nowhere to go from that. Anthony agrees, we hang up, and I go to bed, where I listen to Björk's "Heirloom" on repeat in my headphones until I fall asleep.

65

On Saturday evening Hunter comes over to hang out in Santa Monica because we haven't spent any time together just the two of us in weeks, and I don't think he has anything better to do. First we go down Third Street and walk around the shops. I want to buy a basketball jersey to wear at Coachella, plus a flowery headband to also wear at Coachella with the basketball jersey, because I want to have this combined feminine/bro look, which I came up with because I still think of the story of that Greek teenager who got bullied for being effeminate or gay or something along those lines, and then he went missing for a month, and then they found his body. And I still feel a little bit guilty for perpetuating this stupid heteronormative ideal, where all of us have to act like straight bros all the time and nothing else is acceptable, and I think that maybe being a little bit more explicitly feminine at times wouldn't hurt anyone, and if people have a problem with it, they should come up to me and we can discuss it.

So we go to Urban Outfitters and I buy a vintage Lakers

jersey from 1992 or something and then we go to Tilly's and I try on several flowery headbands in the women's accessories section and decide to go with one that sits on top of your head like a crown and has several little daisies on it. When I'm there doing this, two entry-level cute girls in their twenties come up to me and tell me how good it looks, and I know that they don't mean it, and I know they're making fun of me, but I'm also happy this has happened, because this is exactly the kind of low-stake gay bashing that I expect to happen, and maybe eventually someday people will get used to other people wearing all the daisy headbands they want and acting however the hell they like, and nobody will care.

Then Hunter and I get something to eat at Chipotle and then we go home. At home we just sit around for a bit and listen to some music, a mix of 2Pac and Sky Ferreira, but only the pop years, and we watch part of the film *Fools Rush In* with Salma Hayek and Chandler, but certainly not the whole thing. Then Hunter tells me that, by the way, he's staying over and I say OK, but also ask if he's brought his toothbrush with him, because he's certainly not going to bed without having brushed his teeth. He says that no, he hasn't, and we walk to the store to buy him one. Also I'm running low on toothpaste. It's after eleven thirty at night.

We walk into the grocery store and head to the aisle where one might find the toothbrushes, but as we walk through I catch glimpse of a masc bro in shorts and a T-shirt and a girlfriend, and I think that he's on a lot of steroids currently, so we take a very brief detour to walk past him. Hunter doesn't see the appeal at first, but then after we've been past him and witnessed the size of his arms close by, he agrees that this was a very right decision after all.

Then we're suddenly standing in front of the toothbrushes. Apart from the toothbrush for Hunter, I also have this idea that I need to have a number of new, unopened spare toothbrushes in my bathroom anyway, just in case any other guests want to stay over. In all honesty I stole this idea from a porn star that I slept with a couple of times a few months back. There were always new, unopened toothbrushes at his place, and I really appreciated that.

The cheap toothbrushes that I'm interested in bulk-buying come in packages of two. I look at the whole selection they have and toothbrushes are available in blue, purple, and pink. One package has a blue one and a purple one in it. This is the masc choice. Another package has a purple one and a pink one. This is a very feminine choice. The third package available has a blue one and a pink one. I guess this is a halfway choice. I stop there for a good ten minutes and debate with Hunter which combination of toothbrushes I should purchase. I want to buy four in total. I'm definitely getting the masc choice (blue/purple) but for my other two, I don't know if I should go blue/pink or purple/pink. My concern is that the purple/pink combination might be too feminine for my houseguests and it might put them off. Hunter reminds me that I am now an advocate for feminine gays' right to wear flowery headbands, and I should therefore stick to my newly found convictions, and buy the feminine toothbrush choice. He makes a very valid point, and I walk to the checkout with one masculine and one feminine toothbrush double pack.

Because it's now nearly midnight, there is only one checkout that's open and there's a queue for it, which comprises everyone who's in the store at this time. This serves me very well, of course, because it also includes the steroid guy from the wrong aisle earlier. On a more focused review of the situation, the steroid guy is not very handsome at all, though his muscles remain large. Instead, there is another straight guy with a girlfriend who's queuing right in front of us, and this one is heart-wrenchingly beautiful.

I text Hunter "I'm also interested in this one" followed by an arrow pointing toward him and then Hunter and I spend the next ten minutes staring at the poor guy and praying that the computer malfunction that has immobilized the whole line of people waiting to pay never gets resolved. This guy has an absurdly handsome square-jawed face with stubble, a nose that looks like it may have been broken once in a sports-related accident when he was younger, dark hair, and light blue eyes that are framed by the most distinct hot eyelashes I've ever seen in my life, and you know there's something going on there for real when I feel the need to describe some guy's eyelashes as "hot." He also has an incredible, round, muscular ass that's sticking out in his sweat shorts and an upper body that's never been worked out in his life, which means that his incredible, round, muscular ass just happens to be that way. The girlfriend is a solid 3/10. He must be insane.

Then the checkout starts working again and everyone pays and we all leave and Hunter and I discuss the hot guy from the queue for about half an hour and Hunter is as equally dumbfounded by his beauty as I am, and adds that, yes, he's out of this world, and if he were gay and also went to the gym, he would be a completely perfect, unequivocal 10/10, and I remind Hunter that if the guy was gay he might have gone to the gym and worked his upper body and been a 10/10, but on this Saturday night he would probably also be at some bar in West Hollywood getting wasted or at home crying because of some gay drama/breakup, instead of buying a tub of Ben & Jerry's ice cream with his loving, ugly girlfriend in a remote grocery store in Venice, so he's probably better off this way and we should leave him alone. Then we go home and watch some more TV and fall asleep.

66

On Saturday I have dinner plans with my friend William, who's here in California for the weekend for a work conference. Because of that, I don't feel like I need to make any other plans or see any other people during the day at all. One activity planned is plenty. It's not warm enough to go to the beach, so I stay in bed for a good while, get up just before midday, have breakfast, kill some time buying on Discogs.com old vinyls of albums I used to like when I was a teenager, which will really depress me when they arrive, because the last time I held these records in my hands I was fifteen and I'm sure I had some hopes and dreams and some expectations of how it would all turn out and look at my fucking life now, and then I go to the gym.

When I come back, I get ready to go to this dinner and I even have to make an effort because it's at an expensive restaurant, so I dress like my parents sent me to private school in Switzerland when I was young but they stopped funding me in my early twenties and I haven't reached the age where I'll get access to my trust fund yet, because it's nice to look rich, I'm sure, but if the look is too straightforward and there's no tragedy involved, it's very tacky, I'm sorry, and I leave the house. As I step into my car, I get a call from William and he sounds really sheepish, like he's about to cancel on me and I'll get mad at him, and he cancels on me, but I don't get mad. He and some other guys that he knows here in LA have decided to go down to Palm Springs this weekend instead, there's a White Party happening there, and they want to leave tonight instead of tomorrow morning so they get to all the good daytime parties tomorrow nice and early instead of being stuck in traffic. This plan does make sense. He also asks me if I want to go, but I'm really over it and I don't, so I say have fun and go back to my apartment.

Because it's eight on Saturday night and I have nothing to do and haven't spoken to a real-life person today and now I'm actually bored as fuck and want a quick thrill, I message some guy back that I was talking to on Grindr earlier in the day with no intention to meet. This conversation goes like this:

Me: Hi

Grindr guy: What's up

Me: So, I'm basically free

Grindr guy: Where r u

Me: I'm home in Venice. I don't mind driving over there

Grindr guy: I'll be home around 10. Is that too late

Me: No, that's fine

Grindr guy: Ok. I'll text u once I'm about to arrive home

Me: Should we find out anything else about each other, like our names, what the favorite band we saw at Coachella was, etc., or are we just going by a couple of pictures and straight into it?

Grindr guy: I'm up for anything

Me: Kinda like the idea of turning up without knowing your name

Grindr guy: Let's do it then

Me: aight

Then I send his pictures from Grindr to five of my friends and ask them if anyone knows who he is and two of them text back and say they have hooked up with him and his name is Alex and he is a dentist and he seems like a bit of a spoiled asshole but has a nice apartment and a nice ass and I won't regret it.

Then I wait around and suddenly it's nearly 10:00 P.M. and I text him again and this happens.

Me: Should I set off soon?

Grindr guy whose name is Alex and I pretend not to know that: Hey man I'm really sorry but tonight is not going to work. My friend is having a really odd emergency right now so let's get together another time again sorry

Me: Ah ok. No problem dude

Then I go on Grindr for another couple of hours with no effect, and then I go to bed.

On Sunday I get up late again, because this is my life now,

and wait for Hunter, Peter, and Anthony to come over and pick me up at 2:00 P.M. At 3:00 P.M., they ring my buzzer and I go down.

We go to the beach and walk around and take some pictures and buy some cheap sunglasses and eat some food and then decide to go check out the Venice Canals, because it seems like a fun, low-key activity, and like I said, the weather is not good enough this weekend to hang around on the beach. Also I kinda want to re-create a picture I saw some straight bro post on Instagram where he and a bunch of his friends are sitting on a ledge somewhere and they have their arms over each other's shoulders and they're all casual and shit and it would all be very normal and nice, apart from they have all dropped their pants down to their ankles and are sitting there in their underwear. When I present this idea to the group they're generally up for it, and in fact Anthony recognizes this as an actual thing that people do ("dropping trou," he says, that's what it is), and I'm very excited about the dropping trou concept, apart from the fact that three out of the six of us are not wearing any underwear because I hadn't warned them before, so I'm not sure we can do it.

Anyway, the Venice Canals idea still stands and we go there and walk around and find a bridge that goes over one of the canals and seems pretty chill, plus it's right next to a house where a shirtless bro is working out in his garage with the door open, so we decide to hang there for a while. And this is a bro who's tall and tan and blond, what a surprise, and is wearing only a pair of board shorts and nothing else, and his ass looks beefy and perfect and his body is toned and athletic, but not with a six-pack like a gay guy would have, just the definition and muscle size a normal worked-out straight bro would have, and his feet are completely black from walking around bare-foot everywhere, and he's standing there with another guy (shirted, not hot) and he's doing push-ups and core exercises and pulls-ups and I don't know what else he can do to make me fall in love. Their house seems very rudimentary in decor, in fact the house is pretty tiny and doesn't even seem to have that much furniture in it, with a garage right next to it (where they're working out) and two yards: a fenced one in the back and one right next to the canal with a couple of plastic chairs and a plastic table in it, where they must sit and drink beers after they work out, or so I like to think. They also have a husky roaming around and interrupting their workout and they try to fend him off in a casual, playful way and I kinda want to have their life, to be honest. Well, the hot one's, not the other guy's. Even if they have the same life exactly, I want to have the hot one's life.

Then we're done pretending to chill on the bridge and walk back to the cars and drive off to get some ice cream and on the way to the ice cream I outline my plan to the rest of the group, my plan being:

I will go there on my next day off work in the daytime to whimsically hang out, take a walk on the bridge, maybe ride my bike, check out the scene, bring some treats to their beauti-ful husky, slowly get acquainted with the neighborhood, and eventually ingratiate myself with all the roommates, and this may take weeks or even months, until an opening comes up in the house, someone moves out, and I'm asked to move in. Then, one summer, on a warm Sunday afternoon possibly years from now, they can all come and casually hang on that bridge with me and my bud (and roommate [and lover]), Connor, because that is the name I have assigned him. We'll both have really dirty feet and the husky will come play with him and mostly ignore me, but I will be fine with that.

67

For the upcoming Valentine's Day weekend, Peter and I have decided to go and stay in Miami, seeing that I'll be in New York for work, we have nothing better to do back home in LA, and it's not as warm as Miami there anyway. Plus I've never been to Miami. I finish work with my client in New York on Wednesday and plan to catch a flight to Miami early on Thursday morning, and by early on Thursday morning, I mean at 12:30 P.M., but we all know this means that I have to be at the airport at 11:00 A.M., which means I have to get a cab at 10:15 A.M., which means I have to wake up at 9:00 A.M. to get ready, shower, and eat, and that is an early morning. Peter, who's in D.C. for the week, is planning to meet me late on Friday evening, because he has to wait and catch his flight after work.

Because of this incredibly stressful situation that I find myself in, I decide to take some Xanax for the first time in months just to make sure that I get enough sleep before my flight. I go to bed at midnight and fall asleep pretty much immediately. I wake up around 5:30 A.M. to use the bathroom and take some more Xanax because it worked so well the first time. Then I wake up again at 11:30 A.M. I grab my bags, run down to the street and order an Uber and I'm stupid enough to think that I will still make it, but I must be thinking that I'm somebody else, somebody who turns up at the airport late and is still allowed on the flight, somebody who gets free upgrades by being charming with the check-in staff, that sort of thing. But I am not, so I miss my flight and then take the train back, which takes about an hour, and then I have to book myself back into the hotel because the next flight I could get on is for the same time the following morning.

My revised plan is to hang around, do nothing, maybe go to the gym, then start overdosing on Xanax and sleeping pills early, say around 8:00 P.M., go to bed around 9:00 P.M., which will guarantee that my interrupted sleep cycle will occur earlier, and I'll be up and running by 8:00 A.M. at the latest, guaranteeing that I'll catch my flight. It's foolproof.

I go to the gym around 6:00 P.M. and do legs, and then this kid that I slept with two days ago here in New York turns up and starts working out his back and looking hot as fuck, not necessarily in that order. As always, and this is my biggest failing as a human being, once a hot guy arrives within my visual range all my other functions are paralyzed, my cognitive ability becomes incapacitated, and there's only one thought that my stupid, guy brain is able to form in repeat sequence: I want him so bad, I want him so bad, I want him so bad.

The guy walks up to me and we make casual conversation ("I thought you had left by now," "I missed my flight, I'm such an idiot," etc.) and I think I manage to get through it without even letting my hyperventilating show. Then I text Hunter to tell him what's happening and complain about the paralyzing effect men have on me, then Hunter texts back saying "men = lyfe," and then I continue with my workout.

I'm at the leg press and the guy comes and starts using the lat pull-down machine that's diagonally to my left, only two feet away. We are practically facing each other. He raises his arms and starts pulling the bar down and I'm faced with the fine blond hairs under his arm, which make me sink into my seat and drop my weight. The thing to know about this guy is that he's a trainee lawyer, ten years younger than me, smart, and very attractive. He doesn't need me. I am nothing to him. He can have anyone he wants. I am fully aware of this and I don't begrudge him at all, still I attempt to give it another shot, pick up my phone, and text him.

"You are fuckin gorgeous," I type.

He's actually holding his phone as he receives my text, looks up immediately and smiles at me. I get up and walk away in an attempt to make this less awkward.

He waits several minutes and eventually texts back "Likewise x" with a winking face, while we're in completely different parts of the gym, and this is the final indication that he doesn't really want to talk to me anymore or meet up again before I go away, but he's polite and kind enough to at least text back and let me down gently. I come to terms that this will be the last time we text each other, but he will forever have my heart. I finish my workout, get changed, and leave the gym.

On the way back to the hotel I stop at a restaurant and have dinner on my own. I receive a Snapchat from Anthony back in LA showing a bunch of crumpled-up tissues with a tagline that says "sniff," take my cue, and text him to ask if he's sick.

"Yup—runny nose and cough," he says. "Can't imagine where I picked that up, ha."

"I don't know a final score of how many people you've slept with this week, so I couldn't help you."

"Total = 1. He was sweet enough to share the sniffles."

"How inconsiderate."

"Meh, I'd say it was worth it. How's New York?"

"I missed my flight to Miami, but I'm eating now and had a successful workout, so I'm happy."

"Good—back to bulking?"

"Yes. But I was also sick recently and have lost weight, so I'm not divulging how heavy I am currently."

"Oh come on, how muuuuuuuuuuch?"

"182," I type, and add nine wailing emojis.

"Well that blows. You have plenty of time between now and Coachella, not to worry."

"I suppose that's my real goal, you're right. And my year-end goal is to be 200, which is insane, but we'll see."

"You've been 200 before though, right?"

"No this is the heaviest I've ever been right now. Well, 185 before the sickness."

"Damn, and you want another 15? Someone's greedy."

"I DO. I was 170 this time last year."

"Whaaaa"

"True"

"Impressive though. You'd be a beast at 200."

"I finally want to be someone that matters."

"Yeah get to it will ya? You don't exist if you're under 190."

I tell him that I know and start taking Xanax. Back in the hotel, I fall asleep by 10:00 P.M., wake up in time, and catch my flight to Miami.

68

The first thing I do at JFK airport is check myself in on Facebook to show that I'm traveling to Miami. This has a dual purpose. First of all it adds to the perception that I have this incredible jet-setting lifestyle, where I'm always having fun, always traveling somewhere, and do I even have a job? In fact, chances are that somebody will comment, "Do you ever work," because people love to think on a singular level and only like to do what has been done about sixteen billion times before. It's like when anyone posts a shirtless picture someone will comment, "Do you even own any shirts?" or if the person in the picture has abs, "Eat a sandwich," and they will probably think that such a witticism has never been heard before. The second reason for checking in at the airport is that it says to the people that I'm friends with, even though I don't know who lives in Miami or South Florida, that I'm coming and they should be getting ready to sleep with me.

I get to Miami and take a taxi to the apartment that Peter and I have rented. Because I'm in a new city where I've never been before and because there are many people around that I've never met but have spoken to on Facebook or Instagram and I promised that I would go and meet then, but in fact I'm really too nervous to do that by myself, I stay in the apartment until Peter finally arrives around 8:00 P.M. By that point I'm bored out of my mind, plus I'm now starving because I haven't eaten anything all day, not that this was motivation enough to actually leave, wander around, find somewhere that has food, and talk to the middleman who will sell it to me. Also, because the Wi-Fi in the apartment is working only intermittently, I have reached about 75 percent of the monthly data allowance on my phone, via some really obsessive and very consistent usage of Grindr and Instagram.

Peter arrives and he's full of big plans, as always. We're going to a house party first, but we're also on the guest list for Soho House and, of course, there's an after party for later. The person who has put us on the guest list for Soho House is somebody that Peter met on Grindr on the cab ride between the airport and the apartment, so that's guaranteed to work out. I don't particularly want to go to all this, so I suggest that we go straight to Soho House and skip the first house party, but the deal is that we have to go and meet the Grindr guy at the house party first and head to Soho House together with him, because the guest list thing might not be valid if we go on our own. This all sounds very complicated and I'm not really in the mood to have sex with anyone just to get into Soho House, but Peter reassures me that if anyone needs to put out it will be him, so we get an Uber and go to some ridiculous mansion on the waterfront somewhere in Miami.

The problem with gay guys who attend house parties at

ridiculous mansions on the waterfront in Miami and have Soho House memberships is that they wear nice tucked-in silk shirts, slim-fitting trousers, smart loafers, and Tom Ford fragrances and they're unsexy as fuck. I mean, the dumb, masc musc bros I tend to like are really fucked up and a guarantee for unhappiness, but at least they're hot and don't have blow-dried hair and a keen interest in minimalist interior design and low-carb diets.

At the party I don't really talk to anyone and pretend that I'm quiet because I'm really jet-lagged and just flew in from out of town, and when somebody points out to me that New York and Miami are in the same time zone, I explain that I'm European and didn't actually know that, so my jet-lag excuse still counts, and what is jet lag after all, other than a mental state?

At around 1:00 A.M. we are still there and only now is there talk about moving to Soho House, but there aren't enough drugs and alcohol in South Florida for that to happen for me, so I say good-bye to Peter, order myself an Uber, and go back home to go to bed. Before falling asleep I go through Instagram, of course, where, scrolling through the pictures that people I follow have liked, I see a tall, blond, handsome Canadian guy who seems to also be in Miami for the weekend and who I want to get to know. I follow him and passive-aggressively like a picture of his from several weeks ago showing some graffiti on a wall back where he lives in Toronto, hoping that he will notice me and follow me back. I choose to like the graffiti picture as opposed to a picture of him (of which there are hundreds) for two reasons: (a) to avoid bringing up a picture showing him to my existing followers, so that none of them follow him, and (b) so that he doesn't think I'm that into him, immediately giving him the upper hand. Then I fall asleep.

Peter rolls in at some unidentified time and sleeps on the sofa in the living room instead of climbing into bed with me and disturbing me, which is very nice and considerate of him, although to be fair he's so drunk that in the morning I find him passed out there fully dressed without even using a pillow, just face flat down on the sofa, so I think it was a case of stumbling on the first piece of furniture once he walked in and collapsing there.

69

I like South Beach. You move from London where everyone has a career and some purpose in life to LA and you think, OK, this is quite different, people don't seem to have normal office jobs here, but then you come to South Beach and it seems like nobody has ever worked a single day in their lives. It's quite pleasant. Though I couldn't stand the place for longer than three days.

When I get up on Saturday morning I let Peter sleep while I check messages and get progressively hungry. The blond Canadian guy that I followed on Instagram hasn't followed me back, which is inexplicable to me, and I can only assume that he's playing some sort of game, but I'm only here for another couple of days and we don't have time for this. I look up his name on Facebook and send him a random friend request. Then I'm so hungry that I'm scared I'm losing weight so I wake up Peter and we go to eat.

During all the eating Peter recounts his evening to me and his stories always sound borderline made up, but that's just because he's very candid and provides great detail and these are all things that happen to most of us, but we don't tend to go back and think of, let alone recount, the sequence of events of our sexual encounters in such minute detail. I'm sure any sex act broken down and recited must seem ridiculous in retrospect. On this occasion, Peter met this person at some club where he went, who was an unattractive, older, short British guy, but this guy was really dominant and Peter naturally had no choice but to fall for him. After going upstairs in the club and making out with Peter and making him lick his feet clean, the British guy took Peter home, a hotel actually, because he is also visiting Miami, to continue degrading him. This degradation had to be limited to the bathroom, as the friend the British guy was traveling with was trying to sleep in the same hotel room and didn't want two random people's sexual role-play keeping him up. In the bathroom, the guy presented Peter with a plastic bag that contained a jockstrap and a pair of knee-high athletic socks (all items in bright yellow) and instructed him to put them on. Once Peter was dressed in this attire and nothing else, the guy requested that Peter fall on the floor and gives him twenty push-ups. When this task was also completed, the guy demanded a dance. Not a lap dance, an actual dance. Like the guy was some sort of Middle Eastern king and wanted to be entertained by his harem. With no music on, Peter stood there and danced for a bit in his jockstrap and socks until the guy was satisfied. Then the guy wanted to fuck, but I think the dance thing had killed it for Peter, who then pretended that he'd taken too much G and was about to pass out and therefore had to leave immediately. Then Peter left.

A Facebook notification pops up on my phone followed by a message. The blond Canadian guy has accepted my friend request and has written to me.

He says:

"We know each other?"

I write back:

"I'm afraid we don't. I just randomly added you." I add a sad face emoji to convey self-awareness of how desperate I am. "I think I saw your Instagram."

He replies:

"Oh, thanks for the add. Where u at?"

"I'm in Miami right now, but I live in LA. And you?"

"I'm from Toronto. But in Miami now as well."

"Oh that's awesome."

"Went out last night." He includes two dizzy-looking emojis.

This indicates to me that he takes drugs. I ask:

"Oh yeah? Was it a good time? I just flew in yesterday and was too tired so I went to bed at 1 a.m."

"It was good. If u have time later tonight to have a drink, let me know!"

"Yeah, definitely I will do. I'd like that."

Then he asks me "whatsapp?" and sends me his number and then I text him on Whatsapp. We make loose arrangements to meet later, even though it's very hard to commit to anything with so many boys around.

Peter and I wonder what we should do for the rest of the day until we have to go to the first party at 7:00 P.M. I want to do something cultural that elevates us above all the other gays who go to Miami just to party because we're so clever and wholesome and definitely not like the rest of them, so I suggest that we go check out the Wynwood Art Walk Tour that I found when I was stalking some hot guy's Instagram earlier. Then we realize that this art walk is not in South Beach at all and we'd have to take an Uber for fifteen minutes to get there, so we go to the gay beach instead.

At the gay beach Peter goes and buys four margaritas that come in huge supersize soda-style plastic cups and would be sufficient for at least half a football team post, say, a Super Bowl victory, but he keeps them all to himself. I take an MDMA tablet that Peter found in the club the night before. Or I hope that's what it is anyway. As Peter gets progressively drunk and sloppy, he urges us to stand up and walk around the beach, both so that we can see more people and more people can see us. I am really averse to this idea and generally a very private, reserved person, but I end up going.

The situation on the beach is quite dire, with the exception of three people on several courses of steroids that Peter immediately zones in on. One of them is even blond, so I'm also sold. Peter wants us to go walk past them so that they stop us and talk to us and potentially take him home and tag him. I'm actually not feeling very well as a result of that thing that I took that was definitely not MDMA but I still don't know what it was, and follow him there with a fixed stare on the sand/my feet trying to avoid any human contact, even more so than usual. We walk up to them and they do stop us and Peter makes friendly conversation, which turns very friendly, and I don't know how he does it, because within minutes of talking to anyone, whether in person or online, they become dominant tops and they just want to use him and humiliate him.

The same people are total bottoms when they talk to other people, of course. I suppose it's like when people talk to me and they figure me out pretty quickly and they just pretend to be super masc and play up the whole bro thing, because that's what they realize that I'm into.

In any case, it's not long before two of these three guys have their hands on the back of Peter's neck and are whispering filth into his ear and Peter is lapping it all up and everyone is getting quite hard and I'm getting quite bored, plus my trip has turned into mild—not really unpleasant, but still not hugely enjoyable—catatonia, and I want to go take a nap. Shortly after that we leave, Peter going to some bar with his dom top group and me going home.

Peter comes back to the apartment in a couple of hours and wakes me up. He is very drunk. I make him drink a lot of water so he can sober up and he gives me some coke and a le- gitimate MDMA pill, both of which he acquired from his new friends, who finally proved to be useful in some way. He then insists that he give me a back rub because he says he wants to practice and find new ways to satisfy his tops and I reject this plan immediately on the grounds that it's too sexual between two friends. I have to give myself extra credit for say- ing no to this, even though the MDMA is actually working this time.

A while later we get ready and go out, this time to a bar on Ocean Drive. The incredibly thought-out decoration of bal- loons, banners, and love hearts around the venue remind me that today is Valentine's Day. I am not emotionally advanced enough for this not to bother me and as an immediate, knee- jerk reaction, I text the Canadian guy from Facebook.

I ask him how he is, if he's coming out, and what he's wearing.

He writes back that he's at his friend's house, which is actually just two blocks from the bar where I am, and sends a picture of himself lying facedown on a sofa wearing a pair of green knee-length khaki shorts and white socks. I'm into it. I ask him if he wants to come and say hi and he says that he doesn't feel like going out, he's still tired from the night before, but he'll come and meet me if I like so that we get to see each other in real life.

I get a text twenty minutes later telling me that he's outside the bar. I step outside and see him and I lose my mind, because he's really, really attractive, although I have to admit that I'm really high right now and don't even know what's going on, anyone could have turned up, really. I'm trying to make conversation, but every thought is unfinished and all I know is that I want to leave my friends behind and go home with him. I want to go inside to tell my friends I'm leaving and he says he'd rather wait for me there because he gets way too much attention in gay places and he can't handle it right now, and to be honest I've heard a lot worse from gay men in their twenties, so I don't hold it against him, go inside, say good-bye, and come back out.

He does seem to get a lot of attention from people just as we walk around and this is something very important to me, because I'm an insecure idiot who will never learn. We go to Starbucks; he gets a coffee and I get some water and watch him make flirtatious conversation with the waitress, who is apparently offering to marry him so that he gets a U.S. passport when he tells her he's from Canada. I need to take some sort of therapy that will convince me that being ridiculously good-looking isn't the most important thing there is, even though empirical evidence every day of my life tells me that this is the case.

When we go back to the apartment we start taking our clothes off and he pauses for a second and tells me that he really likes me and he's looking for more than sex, I say yeah perfect, me too, and we get naked. Then, as I lie in bed with this handsome, six two, muscular, blond Viking from Canada, I start thinking of Lloyd. It's been almost a year since he moved out of my place and we've had any sort of extended interaction. I say that I need to use the bathroom, grab my phone, go into the next room, and check Lloyd's Instagram. He's spending the day on the beach. It actually doesn't matter what he's doing. Any action or inaction gives me the same eviscerating feeling that I can't seem to shake off. I go back in the bedroom, have sex with the Canadian, tell him that he can spend the night if he wants but he'll have to stay on his side of the bed, because I can't sleep with people touching me, take 10 mg of Valium, and pass out. The next morning when I wake up, I leave the Canadian sleeping in my bed and go outside. Peter hasn't come home and I haven't heard anything from him.

I guess I'll walk around for a bit and find something to eat. I guess I'll then meet up with Peter, maybe go to the gym, go to some party, and find someone new to give my misguided affection to. And then he'll be gone. Like every day in a different place, sometimes in Berlin, sometimes in London, Los Angeles, and now in Miami, I am alone, and the thoughts that form inside my head take over my surroundings. Because everything means too much, and despite the passing of time, nothing ever goes away. And if I were to reflect, try to come up with any sort of life assessment and see what it is that I contributed to the world, the answer would be this: stories about how desirable I tried to be, how beautiful everyone around me was, and how damaged I had become, handing the world back pieces of my broken self.

Acknowledgments

Mum and Dad, for making sure that I'm never really scared of anything and I don't depend on anyone. My sister, for somehow believing that I'm better than I actually am.

Paul Burston and Bobby Nayyar, the first people who took action to put my words in print.

James Melia, a great, perceptive editor whose enthusiasm and vision helped shape this book.

There would be no book without John Hein, Brett, and Michael. I had forgotten for a while what I can do. Thank you for reminding me.

Llwyd, always.

Thanks also to the following people for your friendship, support, and advice: Mitchell Bederman, Will Brereton, Antonio Casanez, Alex Charvalias, Lisa Culligan, Daniel De Castro, Andrea de Lugnani, Rus Eltman, Peter Evans, Neil Jaworski, Carrie Lawrence, Vasilios Mantoulidis, Michael Murphy, Robin Sanderson, Jeremy Schiestel, Mark Waterston, and James Zazzali.